£2.95

THE LIF

'A professional always comes prepared, ... secure in the certainty that he was every inch the professional, whatever anybody else said.

The sea was turning choppy and the wind began to rise. He scarcely felt the cold through the wet suit, but he could feel it on his face and on his hands, the chill and the spray, bringing unwelcome thoughts of lonely peril and souls lost to the waves.

The lights of the buoys rose and fell but seemed to come no nearer. Geraint hunched lower, cutting his wind resistance, willing the boat to go faster. The wind and the wet and the time it would take – they were all part of the same thing, he reminded himself. They were all components of adversity, and nothing was achieved without adversity. He made himself bare his teeth at the night as his mind ran the same phrase over and over, his talisman against the frightening dark:

I am the master of my fate, I am the captain of my soul . . .

Lynda La Plante was born in Liverpool in 1946 and now lives in Surrey. She trained as an actress at RADA and worked in cabaret, musicals and the theatre, including the Royal Shakespeare Company and the National Theatre. She also worked in films and television before turning to writing. Her TV series, which include *Widows, Civvies* and *Framed*, have won her international acclaim; she is also the author of four bestselling novels, *The Legacy, The Talisman, Bella Mafia* and *Entwined.*

Also by Lynda La Plante
and available in Mandarin

Prime Suspect 2
Prime Suspect 3
Widows 2
Framed
Civvies

THE LIFEBOAT

LYNDA LA PLANTE

Mandarin

A Mandarin Paperback

THE LIFEBOAT

First published in Great Britain 1994
by Mandarin Paperbacks
an imprint of Reed Consumer Books Ltd
Michelin House, 81 Fulham Road, London SW3 6RB
and Auckland, Melbourne, Singapore and Toronto

A CIP catalogue record for this title
is available from the British Library
ISBN 0 7493 1791 4

Printed and bound in Great Britain
by Cox & Wyman Ltd, Reading, Berks

Lynda La Plante would like to thank Jessica Pope and the cast of actors who have suffered many hardships in the filming of the series, but have retained their good humour and professionalism.

The *Lifeboat* production team would like to express their sincere thanks to the RNLI for their encouragement and co-operation in the making of the television series.

Late sunlight shimmered gold on the water as a small fishing boat chugged towards the harbour with an escort of bitching gulls. At the sides fishermen worked steadily, drawing in the green nets, cheerful and noisy at the end of another trip.

Deep in the murk below the boat a barnacled wreck swayed on a stray current. A fishing net trailed across its top, dislodging a tangle of wire and the twisted panels of a cabin door. Shards and fragments rose in a silent flurry as the net unbalanced a cluster of spongy planks, setting free a dark metal sphere, heavily rusted. It rolled out from a crevice in the wreck and rotated upwards through the gloom. Beneath it a massive buoy sprang free and jerked to a stop three feet below the surface, held on a taut, blackened rope.

A man working in the bows stopped and peered across the water, seeing fragments glint on the surface, silvery and green.

'Starboard,' he called to the wheelhouse. 'There's something adrift.'

The boat's engine died and a second man came to the side with a hooked pole. He leaned out over the water and poked at the debris. A few yards away the rusted, spiked sphere rose with a whoosh, half tangled in the net.

The man with the pole jumped back. His mouth opened and closed twice before he found his voice.

'It's a bloody mine!' he yelled, turning, flailing his arms. 'Get the hell out! Skipper! It's a mine!'

Frantically the men cut the nets, slashing the cords as the engine surged to life. The laden nets sank as the boat turned in a tight sweep, its propellers pounding the water to foam.

The fishermen hunched together at the stern, watching the debris drift back on their wake, the big malignant mine, net-tangled at the centre, bobbing like a hellish beach ball. Splintered wood cushioned the mine as it bumped against the rocks. It bounded back a couple of feet and did a half spin, bobbing, then rolled forward, hitting the pulpy wood again. Water squelched from the debris as the mine rebounded a second time, rolled and was carried forward suddenly against bare rock. It clanked sharply.

For a moment everything seemed to freeze. The fishermen stopped breathing. Then the mine exploded, an orange flash and a fearsome bang, splitting rock, throwing up a curtain of water and putting a shudder through the joists of the fishing boat.

The fishermen looked at each other, their faces soaked. Fifty yards away, beyond the place where flotsam showered down in pieces smaller than peas, the sea rumbled. Bubbles hissed to the surface in an oily stream as the hulk below the waves settled back into its silted crater.

1

The scream of the circular saw drowned the bleeping pager in Leslie Parry's belt. The noise filled the old workshop, where fine sawdust hung like pollen in the warm air.

'I've never had an apprentice yet that could use this old bugger.' Leslie addressed the remark to Pete Pugh, who was halfway across the yard. 'Steady, now, steady . . .' He shifted his grip on the plank as chips flew around his head and bounced off his goggles. 'Got to keep your eye on the grain of the wood . . .'

Leslie was big and powerfully built, a man with an intelligent, good-natured face that invoked respect the instant it stopped looking friendly. He was a hard worker though not fanatical about it, he had a tendency to think out loud, and occasionally he talked a lot older than his years. In Penrhys he was no longer an oddity, they were used to the big fair-haired bloke who looked Scandinavian, but was really Irish, and happened to live on the South Wales coast.

'Les . . .'

Pete Pugh eased a length of four-by-four off his shoulder and propped it by the workshop door. He turned off his pager and waved it at Leslie.

'Les!' he stepped closer and shouted louder. 'Les!'

Leslie looked up and saw him. He turned off the

saw and pushed up his goggles. As the motor faded the sound of his bleeper surfaced. He turned it off and stared at Pete.

'Why didn't you tell me?'

He threw off his safety gloves and strode to the yard gate.

'Nobody touch that saw,' he warned a couple of labourers at the back of the yard. 'Turn it off at the mains, lad.'

Pete grabbed his jacket and did as he was told, loathing the dogsbody slot he filled around here, hating the way he sometimes caught himself getting used to it. He pulled on his jacket and ran out of the yard. Leslie was astride his old Harley Davidson and wearing the scuffed, studded leather jacket that looked as old as the bike itself. He jammed on his helmet and zipped up his gloves as Pete clambered on the back.

'Right?'

'Right!'

Leslie turned the key and the engine fired. The bike growled off down the lane, heading for the coast road and the lifeboat station. At the corner they passed Ernie Hardy, running too fast for a fat man. His wind-cheater, worn over his police uniform, flapped in the wind as he clumped along on his rubber-soled boots. He waved to Leslie and yelled breathlessly that he was on his way. He also yelled – because it was his duty, and not because he thought he would be heard – that Pete ought to be wearing a helmet.

In Penrhys, meanwhile, the Regal's matinee of *Lethal Weapon 3*, part of the grand *Lethal Weapon* re-run season, had just been killed off part-way into the second reel. As thirty-two disgruntled punters asked each other what was up, the young proprietor Gwilym Davies, who was also the projectionist, was leaving by the side door, pulling on his donkey jacket as he went. Behind him came Gladys, box-office attendant and usherette, looking harassed. She was a woman out of her time, sallow-skinned from too little daylight, wearing the kind of skirt and blouse they wore in films like *Mrs Miniver*.

'Give them their money back, Gladys,' Gwilym called over his shoulder, 'or tell them to keep the stubs and come in next matinee.' The pager on his belt started bleeping again. He fumbled with it, trying to hit the switch. 'Leave the keys in the usual place, and lock the ice-cream fridge.'

At the George Hotel in the centre of town, the proprietor George Bibby had just left for the lifeboat station, mustering some drama by letting his pager go on bleeping as he hurtled out of the bar followed by the bank manager, Edward Thorpe. George's wife Barbara came to the front of the bar as the door banged shut behind them. She put her newspaper on the bar and smiled wearily.

'It's all right, it's not an emergency,' she told Meryl, the barmaid. 'Just a training thing.'

David Thomas, a local journalist, rushed in and stood mouth-breathing by the bar, pushing his hair back from his forehead. He looked anxiously from one woman to the other, as if their expressions might tell him something. He finally asked Barbara if George had gone.

'You'll maybe catch him out in the car park with Mr Thorpe.'

Thomas hurried out, faster than he had come in.

Barbara watched him go, absently patting both sides of her shagpile perm. She picked up the fresh gin and tonic Meryl had put in front of her. 'He's desperate for a scoop, poor love,' she said. 'Remember that fire on the caravan site? Big drama. And he was in bed with a migraine . . .'

Barbara stiffened noticeably as her son appeared by the passage at the side of the bar. Rufus Myers-Lloyd was with him. Young women found Rufus desperately handsome. A few of the older ones, topped-up on oestrogen, made open advances to him. *He's got a dazzling, aristocratic charm* – one of them had actually said that after three vodka martinis. Barbara thought Rufus was an oily double-barrelled con man, and most likely a degenerate into the bargain. He was certainly the wrong company for her son.

'Steve.' Her voice came out more metallic than she had intended. 'Steve!'

He made an elaborate show of drooping his shoulders before he came over. He was at that age, all blotchy skin and overdone gestures. Rufus called a polite greeting to Barbara, but he stayed at the end of the passage, radiating his affable smile. Barbara nodded to him stiffly, as if her neck hurt. When Rufus spoke to Meryl she smiled shyly and blushed.

'You're lucky your dad's not here,' Barbara hissed at Steve. 'You know he doesn't want you mixing with him.'

'He just wants to borrow some tapes.'

'So long as that's all he wants. Go on, get rid of him.'

Steve and Rufus went off to the living quarters.

'He's back then,' Meryl said, living up to her reputation for stating the obvious.

'Yes.' Barbara shook out the paper, revealing the headline EXPLODING MINE ROCKS SHORELINE. 'He's back. More's the pity.'

Out on the coast road, Leslie Parry was pushing the Harley over the speed limit and thinking this must have been how it was in the old days, whenever hairy little Taffs gathered to beat back invaders from their borders. Volunteers were coming from all directions, converging on the lifeboat station, submitting to the powerful impulse that made Welshmen group and do things together – drinking, fighting, playing rugger, saving lives.

Leslie overtook an immaculate old black Rover driven by Edward Thorpe, bank manager and Penrhys Lifeboat Honorary Secretary. In the back David Thomas was catching his breath while George Bibby, sitting up front, hung out of the window barracking every volunteer they passed.

At the lifeboat station the mechanic, Hughie Jones, was already swaddled in his yellow and orange protective clothes, impatient to be away. He was a man somewhere in his forties, compactly built with a gentle-featured, marginally dour face weathered by years of contact with the sea. He waved from the boathouse as Leslie Parry and Pete Pugh reached the bottom of the cliff steps.

'Any idea which inspector we've got coming?' Leslie asked him. 'If it's Penrose he'll be on our side, he's a good bloke.'

Hughie agreed with that, but he thought it might be Penrose's new deputy, Spooner.

'Well . . .' Leslie shrugged, determined to make a virtue of the unavoidable. 'If it's him, he'll be trying to prove himself. So we best put up a good show.'

Leslie and Pete hurried through to the changing room beside the ramp, where the lifeboat stood tethered by the winch. Other volunteers were already there, clambering into their protective outfits. As soon as Edward Thorpe arrived he took hold of his shield of authority, the clipboard. His function here was administrative, since he had too much bureaucratic dignity and excess bodyweight to go out with the lifeboat. He checked with Hughie that they had clearance from the Coastguard, then strutted around the boathouse, calling names and ticking off those present.

At the top of the cliff steps a police panda car drew up and Inspector Barry Mitchell leapt out. Apart from being the most senior police officer for miles, he was the assistant mechanic on the lifeboat. As he made for the steps PC Ernie Hardy came thrashing along on his bike. He jumped off and ran down the steps after Barry, catching up with him half-way down. They talked as they clattered their way to the bottom.

'You must have got a right move on,' Ernie panted, making it sound like an accusation. 'You going out with the boat, then?'

Barry glared at him. They were both young men, but Barry had a few years' edge and a sterner face, which sat well with his rank. 'You're on duty in an hour, Ernie. Any road, I was here first.'

Ernie took it mutely, although he looked hurt. 'Does anything need my urgent attention then?' he asked. 'Or can I just hang around here?'

They reached the bottom of the steps and Barry ran

to the boathouse. Ernie sat down and lit a cigarette.

Activity inside the boathouse was organised commotion. Leslie, who was the coxswain, was half-way into his waterproofs and conferring with Edward Thorpe about which of the volunteers should go out with the boat. Men going to sea would be paid expenses and Thorpe had to make a careful list. When they had agreed the selection Leslie finished changing, ran up the steps and got on the boat. George Bibby climbed on after him, followed by David Thomas, the second coxswain.

Edward Thorpe came to the top of the steps, waving his pen to draw attention to himself. 'Right everybody, can I . . .' He coughed and waved the pen higher in the air. 'Can I have your attention?'

The bustle continued. Leslie asked loudly if anybody had seen any sign of the District Inspector yet.

'Lads,' Thorpe shouted, still trying to get their attention. 'Lads, as you all know, this is just a call-out for the benefit . . . *Quieten down*!' He coughed again, gesturing with the ballpoint. '. . . for the benefit of the District Inspector. But treat it as an emergency. Take it seriously . . .'

He suddenly realised he had lost the top off his pen. He spun about, looking for it, then jumped with shock as Chris Spooner, the Deputy District Inspector, came up through a hatch on the lifeboat. He was fully dressed in his protective clothes. He nodded coolly to Thorpe, thumbed his stopwatch and noted the time it had taken to prepare for the launch. Leslie Parry glanced at his own watch and winked at Hughie. They had made decent time.

'Ready for service,' Leslie said sharply.

Spooner nodded.

'Get her off the chains!' Leslie yelled.

The winch turned slowly, drawing the boat back a foot, putting slack in the retaining chains. One of the shore crew pulled the heavy links clear and another stood by, holding a sledge-hammer at the ready.

'Fire her up!'

The engines churned to life, filling the boathouse with noise.

'Knock her off!'

The sledge-hammer banged down on the holding pin. It flew clear with a crack and the boat went gliding down the slipway.

Deckchair Jones, an elderly devotee, came forward and stood by Edward Thorpe, watching big symmetrical waves fan out and break across the bows as the boat cut into the water. For a moment it appeared to sink, then it surged up, spilling torrents, riding the waves. Deckchair moved closer to Thorpe, absently stroking his beard. 'Look at that,' he murmured. 'Perfect.'

Thorpe smiled. It was a straightforward, unexceptional launch, but Deckchair had the enthusiasm of a child.

'Will the DI keep them out there for long?'

'As long as it takes.'

Deckchair watched the rise and fall of the boat as it ploughed its way across the harbour. Over the years the old man had become a partial fixture here, practically a mascot. When he wasn't attending to the deckchairs and sun umbrellas on the front he could be found in the boathouse, doing odd jobs or watching other people do theirs.

'What about the lads?' Deckchair nodded towards the shore crew.

'They can relax for an hour at least.' Thorpe turned and went back into the boathouse. 'Would you tell them for me?'

Deckchair nearly lost his balance as Geraint Gower shoved past him, obviously in a temper. He charged up the stairs after Thorpe. 'Just like his bloody father before him,' Deckchair muttered.

Geraint strode into the crew room. 'I want to talk to you, Edward Thorpe!'

Thorpe sat at the desk and instinctively picked up a pen. He stared at Geraint with eyes magnified balefully by his glasses. He wondered how many times he had seen that look on Geraint's face, the petulant scowl of the habitual moaner, the downturned mouth framed and exaggerated by the beard and moustache. With those crazy eyes and prominent cheekbones, Thorpe mused, Geraint looked like Lenin with curly hair.

'This is the third time in a row I've not been picked and I want to know why!' Geraint slapped the desk for emphasis. 'You got something against me, then come out with it!' He held up his right hand, a stiff trident. 'Three times now . . .'

'Calm down, man,' Thorpe said. 'This is not an emergency, it's just an inspection.'

'Bloody important one, though!'

'We lined up the best crew in the fastest time. If you have any complaints –'

'I got a complaint, all right. I'm being bypassed! Third time!' Three fingers came up again. 'Leslie Parry is doing it on purpose.'

'Now, now, that's ridiculous!' It was Thorpe's turn to put on a face, the stern-but-appeasing one he used for farmers when they panicked about sky-high interest rates. 'We want no ill-feeling, especially not now.'

Geraint's expression went from irate to huffy, then to sly. 'And maybe I got some information on Aberceri,' he said, his voice softer now, the gentle bringer of lousy news. He paused for effect. 'They're confident they'll get the big boat. So if they do, we'll get lumbered with the inflatable.'

'Now then . . .' Thorpe sat back sharply, making his jowls wobble. 'Don't you go spreading rumours. Nothing has been decided. And I should know. I am the Honorary Secretary, Geraint, and as such –'

'As such you know bugger all!' Geraint shouted, banging open the door and striding out of the room.

'Pennant Coastguard, Pennant Coastguard . . .' In the wheelhouse David Thomas addressed the radio slowly and clearly, leaning close to the mike as the boat rose and fell. 'This is Penrhys Lifeboat, this is Penrhys Lifeboat on exercise, repeat on exercise. Crew list is one, two, five, six, seven, eight and ten, accompanied by the Deputy DI . . .'

At the rail Leslie Parry stood next to Spooner, who was managing to look detached from the proceedings. He consulted his watch again as Leslie took the opportunity to slip in a promotional point. 'You can see why Penrhys should have a big boat,' he said. 'Nasty currents along this stretch of shore, and –'

'Can we continue up the coast?' Spooner asked, icy faced. 'Then I'd like to see the crew in action.'

Leslie nodded and went back to the wheelhouse. Hughie Jones came in and stood beside him as he took the wheel.

'I reckon it's still between us and Aberceri,' Leslie

said. 'He's giving nothing away. I just wish we had a ruddy crisis, let us really show him . . .'

Something jarred low in the vessel, shaking it, a thump followed by a rasping that could be felt more than heard. It vibrated in the wheel under Leslie's hands.

'What the hell was that?' He looked at Hughie. 'There's nothing charted around here.'

'It's like something coming from underneath us.' Hughie peered over David Thomas's shoulder. 'Anything on the screen?'

At that moment, without being seen by anyone in the wheelhouse, Deputy Inspector Spooner fell overboard. He was in the water only seconds before Gwilym Davies saw him flailing in the waves.

'Man overboard! Man overboard!'

Leslie threw the engines into neutral as David ran out on deck to help the crew, who were already into the rescue procedure. Manoeuvring the boat in low gear, Leslie sidled it to where Spooner was bobbing in the water. Pete Pugh and George Bibby hung over the side, ready to grab him. As their hands touched his shoulders he brought up his watch and thumbed the button.

'The little bugger!' Leslie hissed.

Back at the boathouse, having completed his few small duties, Edward Thorpe stood in sullen conversation with Constable Ernie Hardy and Doc Lewis, the local GP. They were at the big open doors, staring westward across the water. Behind them Deckchair Jones stood polishing a brass bell, giving his hands something to do as he listened to familiar ground being trodden all over again.

'I don't believe it,' Ernie said. 'I mean, there's been

a big boat at Penrhys for seventy years, and yet, we get an *inflatable* and . . .' He shook his head. 'They only take three crew.'

Doc Lewis was staring dreamily at the sunlight flashing on the waves. He was a dapper man, balding and moustached, with a firm jaw and hard, clear eyes. Nearly forty years before, as a student, he had been told by a professor of morbid anatomy that he had the eyes of a born diagnostician.

'It'll be the end of an era.' He managed to sound defeated and combative at the same time; as the official Medical Officer to the lifeboat crew he felt as personally involved in the forthcoming decision as any of the volunteers. 'Have Aberceri had more call-outs than us, at all?' he asked, clutching at a very slender straw.

Thorpe didn't know, so he ignored the question. He nodded at the map tacked on the boathouse wall behind them. 'You can see there would be no need for all three stations to have a fast, all-weather boat.' He turned his finger in a small circle, signifying the cluster of St Margaret's, Penrhys and Aberceri. 'St Margaret's have been allocated one, that we know, and if it's Aberceri instead of us . . .'

Ernie watched Thorpe frown. 'Do you know something, Mr Thorpe?'

'No.' Thorpe looked offended, which he was good at doing. 'Not at all. You know very well it'll be weeks before we're told.'

'Three crewmen,' Ernie groaned. 'How would they deal with something like that ferry disaster?'

Deckchair bonged the brass bell. They looked at him. 'Took thirty on board,' he said reverently, his eyes wide. '*Thirty*!'

'He's right,' Ernie said, as if the others didn't know. 'Thirty rescued. I mean that's got to go down as a big plus for us, hasn't it, Doc?'

Lewis shrugged delicately. 'That was a few years back now, mind, and –'

'What are we supposed to be doing?' Ernie demanded. 'Picking up swimmers? A small inflatable would bounce around like a rubber ball.'

Deckchair was on his feet, shading his eyes, seeing the shore crew move towards the ramp. 'The lads are coming back, Mr Thorpe.'

'And there's trouble,' Thorpe grunted, pointing. 'Bloody Geraint Gower.'

Gower was following the shore crew, waving his arms, haranguing them.

'Last thing we need is him shooting his mouth off to the DI,' Thorpe said. 'Get him in here.'

In the end it was hopeless. When Geraint got his dander up he could not be contained. Any attempt to divert or thwart him was a squandering of energy. As the boat was eventually winched back into position on the ramp and the crew came down the steps, Geraint was waiting. He buttonholed Spooner like a starving man after a hand-out. 'I'd like to know', he declaimed loudly, 'if the RNLI feel that on a call-out, be it exercise or emergency, every volunteer should by rights get an opportunity to put his training into practice . . .'

Spooner walked away sharply to examine the winch drum. Geraint went after him. 'I've not been used for the last three call-outs,' he said, raising his voice. 'I'm unemployed, but I've got more experience than –'

'Geraint!' Thorpe yelled, surprising himself. 'Shut up, will you?'

Having managed to state the gist of his case, Geraint suddenly allowed himself to be suppressed. He skulked away, hands in his pockets, muttering, leaving the Deputy DI to his thin-lipped scrutiny of the winching gear.

Elsewhere in the boathouse, post-exercise procedures were set in train and by stages the station began to look exactly the way it had before the boat went out. In the final stages Barry Mitchell approached Leslie, who was obviously in a hurry to leave. 'What do you think it was that bumped us, Les? Felt like it was coming from under the boat.'

Leslie, distracted, scribbled something on the DI's check sheet, then looked questioningly at Barry, who decided not to repeat himself. He registered a complaint instead.

'You know one of your lads plumbed in the washer-dryer? Well, we're not getting any hot water.'

Leslie had moved away again to say something to Spooner. He turned back to Barry and nodded. 'It's in the books for tomorrow. But with the call-out today I've had my hands full and now I'm quite a bit behind, so be patient, eh?'

Leslie held up the keys for the equipment store and rattled them at Hughie, who was leaning over by the boat, examining the underside of the hull. 'Keys, Hughie.'

Leslie threw them and turned away. Hughie reached out with both hands. The keys sailed past him and clanked on to the floor. Hughie looked around the boathouse for a moment, checking the hubbub, making sure nobody had noticed. He turned and saw the keys in a corner. He went over and bent to pick them up, then straightened sharply, rubbing his eyes. For a minute he stood still, squinting and blinking, not trusting himself to move. Behind him he heard Leslie leaving.

'I'll go and finish off the reports,' Leslie called out, addressing anyone who could hear him.

As he hurried off Barry grinned and winked at Gwilym Davies. 'We all know where he's heading. "Finish off the reports" – that's a new name for it.'

Gwilym frowned, eyes averted, gesturing with small jerks of his head. Barry turned and saw Pete Pugh glaring at him. Barry's grin faded. 'Just a joke, Pete. No harm meant.'

'None taken,' Pete said, smothering his anger.

2

A Range Rover, decorated with mobile-disco posters, giving off muffled bass-thudding music, raced along the winding road north of Penrhys and turned in through the high gates of the Myers-Lloyd property. It braked by the flaking frontage of the rambling manor house, and as Rufus Myers-Lloyd turned off the music young James ran up, brandishing a toy gun. The boy adopted a wide-legged stance and raised the barrel of the gun as Rufus jumped down from the cab.

'Gonna blow you away, man,' James drawled, a steel-eyed, ten-year-old killer.

'Oh, no, no, wait . . .' Rufus stiffened, drawing his long leather coat about him, pushing back the leather cowboy hat. He licked his lips nervously and put up his hands. 'I'm the Lone Ranger. Please don't shoot . . .'

'I warned you!' James snarled, lowering his blond head, preparing to fire. 'You had it comin'!'

He squeezed the trigger. The gun clicked twice. Rufus lurched against the side of the Range Rover, clutching his chest.

As he slid to the gravel Lady Myers-Lloyd appeared from the porched gate leading to the side of the house. She looked displeased. 'Rufus! I told you I needed the car. Do you know what time it is?'

'No!' Rufus begged as James stepped close to him,

aiming the gun again. 'No, *please*!'

James fired again, a volley of clicks. Rufus leapt to his feet and grabbed the small boy, turning him upside down. 'I told you! Never shoot an unarmed man!'

Lady Myers-Lloyd pointed at the Range Rover. 'I want those stickers removed,' she snapped. '*Now*, Rufus. And then I want words with you.'

She was a lean, attractive, clear-eyed woman, the kind who never really age; at that moment her delicate jaw was thrust forward and she looked capable of striking her son. 'Are you listening to me?' she demanded.

Rufus paused with James half-way across his shoulder. He made a show of remembering what she had said. 'Stickers off the windows, right.' He turned James upright and set him on the ground. 'You heard the boss. Let's get those wanted posters out and into the Sheriff's office . . .'

Lady Myers-Lloyd turned away and stamped back along the path to the house. 'Rufus,' she called, 'inside. Now!'

He followed her into the house. She went straight to the kitchen and picked up her handbag. Rufus opened the fridge and took out a bottle of milk.

'There was a fifty pound note in my purse this morning,' she said.

Rufus took the milk to the table and sat down. He put the bottle to his lips and swallowed several times, staring at her. 'There *was* a fifty pound note, yes,' he said, wiping his mouth. 'You also told me to get petrol, so –'

'The change, then, please. Give me the change.'

'I got some petrol, then I dropped in at the George, I owed Steve Bibby a few quid and he nabbed me . . .'

Lady Myers-Lloyd stared at her son, seeing his father, the same patrician, faintly arrogant set of his features, the same veiling of the eyes when he lied. She stepped closer to him. 'Look at me,' she said, and waited until he raised his head and met her stare. 'I can't deal with it, Ru. If you are back on it . . .'

'I'm straight, for Christ's sake!' Rufus gulped more milk, splashing his knuckles. He looked at his mother again, his face softening. 'I've got some gigs to sort out for tonight,' he said, 'there's a few parties, they've asked for the disco. Steve and I needed to get some tapes made.'

'Well, it'll have to wait.' Lady Myers-Lloyd snapped her handbag shut, becoming brisk again. 'I need you to stay with James. Phyllis has gone to look after her sister, she's ill again.'

'What time is Phyllis back?'

'I just told you, she's at Vera's. She always stays over, that's why I need you here.'

'Well!' Rufus glared indignantly at his mother. 'That really buggers up my night! I need the car. You tell me to get work, I get it, and –'

'Just stay with James until I get back. I need *my* car.'

'What for?'

'If you must know, it's a possible buyer for the house.'

'So you still want to sell up?' He shook his head. 'The old man wouldn't have wanted you to part with the family inheritance.' Rufus said it with an ironic whine, since his father hadn't cared a damn about tradition.

'Maybe he should have thought about the family before he bankrupted us.'

'Well, at least he died happy.'

'And drunk.'

They glared at each other. Rufus got up and shoved back the chair. 'Is it all right if I use the phone? I'll pay you for the call.'

Lady Myers-Lloyd rolled her eyes. Rufus went to the hall and she followed him. 'Who are you calling?'

He spun on her angrily. 'Stop checking on my every move! It's driving me nuts!'

His mother looked hurt. He relented and folded his arms about her. 'I'm sorry,' he said, calm again, every inch as smooth as his father. 'Just had a few things to arrange, but I'll stay home, don't worry.'

'I do worry, and I don't mean to harp on at you, but money is tight all round, Ru. I think sometimes you forget James is yours, I don't even have his school fees for next term.'

'I don't forget he's all mine,' Rufus said. He released his mother gently and stepped back. 'But it was your idea to have him here.'

She looked astonished. 'He's your *son*. I wouldn't let anyone else have him, how could you even say that?'

'I didn't mean it the way it came out. You know how much I appreciate what you do for him.'

James appeared from the hall, moving tentatively, testing the air the way children do. They both smiled at him. Rufus kissed his mother's cheek. 'Who loves you?' he murmured, then took her gently by the shoulders and guided her to the door. 'Go on, you go. Me and Clint Eastwood here will start frying up.'

Lady Myers-Lloyd left them. Rufus listened to the door close, then cursed under his breath. He snatched up the telephone and poised his finger over the buttons.

'Who are you calling?' James said.

'Oi,' Rufus warned, 'don't you start. Just piss off into the kitchen and get the frying pan on and the oven-ready chips out.' He began tapping the buttons. '*Now*, James!'

A mile away to the south west, in the marital home of Vera and Leslie Parry, Vera was at that moment standing by the telephone table with the receiver pressed to her ear. As her sister Phyllis walked in she muttered something into the mouthpiece, then replaced the handset and dropped back heavily into her wheelchair. Without a word of greeting she wheeled herself across the over-furnished living-room and picked up a shopping list. She spun the chair and looked at her sister.

'I'm sick to death of all these calls,' she announced in her reedy, burr-edged voice. 'Leslie never says no to a job he's offered – I daren't show my face, there's half the town with half a job done. That Mrs Evans . . .' She pointed at the telephone, shaking her head, 'she's got half a roof. I felt like saying to her, "That's nothing, I've got half a porch extension." '

Phyllis made an effort to look sympathetic, but her heart wasn't in it. She had a bleak and hard enough life of her own, without shelling out compassion for her sister's self-pity, or her come-and-go paralysis, or her travesty of a marriage. The only emotion Phyllis could feel towards Vera, with any force, was guilt, and only occasionally, when she realised that although she herself had arrived at middle age with precious little in the way of emotional or material bounty, her poor maladjusted heap of a sister had even less.

'I've made out a list,' Vera said, brandishing the slip of paper. 'Get some of that nice lavender spray polish too, will you?' She looked round the room, the tip of her tongue sliding along her thin lips. 'Everywhere needs a good *dusting*.' She handed Phyllis the list. 'I've got some ironing ready for you.'

She aimed her chair at the hall and wheeled forward. As often happened, her judgement was out and she hit the door frame. She cursed gutturally then sat silent, staring at the hall carpet. Her head jerked round suddenly.

'You know they're going to get rid of the lifeboat?'

Phyllis looked shocked. 'Get rid of it? Why?'

'They're replacing it. If they get one of them small dinghy things, Leslie'll have no excuse for spending all his time at the boathouse.'

'Not all his time,' Phyllis said airily.

Vera's mouth twisted. 'Phyllis,' she said, 'I can always depend on you to hit where it hurts.'

Later, when the shopping and the ironing were done and the evening was drawing on, Phyllis went round closing the windows and turning up the radiators. Vera was parked in her chair in front of the television. Phyllis poured a glass of sherry and took it to her.

'Will Leslie be home? Only the lifeboat's back, I saw Dr Lewis when I was out.'

'Frank? You saw him?' Vera shook her straight hair girlishly, clasping the schooner with both hands. 'Did he ask after me?' Her eyes were drawn back to the TV screen. She sighed. 'It's a terrible thing, Phyllis, to have taken the wrong road in life. I think worse than anything is knowing you've taken it.'

Phyllis shifted uneasily. Her sister's syrupy regrets, powered more by imagination than by fact, were hard to take.

'Most people', Vera went on, 'don't know, they don't even think about it. But being the way I am, I think about it all the time. I should never have got married again.'

'You should count yourself lucky,' Phyllis told her. 'Two husbands! I've never had one.' She went to the door and paused. 'But if you hadn't thought you were pregnant you might not have got Leslie.'

Vera, suddenly furious, snatched up a cushion and threw it. Phyllis dodged out into the hall, giggling.

Leslie Parry let himself in at Bronwen Pugh's back door. She was getting her twin daughters ready for bed when he tiptoed along the passage and poked his head round the side of the door. He smiled and held up a bottle of wine.

'God, have you got something to celebrate, Les? Come in, I'll be with you in a minute.' She turned to the girls, told them to have sweet dreams and kissed them both. 'Night night, now . . .'

She stepped into the hallway and watched the girls go up to bed. Leslie got the corkscrew from a drawer and paused, looking at her. He felt his chest swell. In another age Bronwen would have been called buxom: she was a ripe-figured woman with a bright, open, youthful face and an abundance of red hair that fell to her shoulders in luxuriant waves. Standing there in her prosaic jeans and checked shirt, half smiling as she bade the girls good-night again, she embodied Leslie Parry's entire notion of compelling, no-nonsense femininity.

She turned and came into the kitchen. 'Pete's not back yet,' she said.

Leslie gave the corkscrew three turns and pulled.

The cork came out with a soft plop. 'He's a good lad, Bron.' He put the wine on the table. 'But he's a bloody useless carpenter. I thought you said he was good with his hands? He's no better at plastering . . .'

'Well, he was a fisherman,' Bronwen said. 'It'll take a while. He's willing, God bless him, and he's up all hours, studying engineering.'

Leslie got two glasses. 'We put up one hell of a show this afternoon,' he said. 'If anyone deserves the big boat . . .'

'I hear Aberceri think the same.'

'They don't stand a chance.' Leslie poured the wine. It was a young Spanish red with a fruity aroma. He handed Bronwen her glass and sniffed at the rim of his own. 'I'm confident.'

'You must be,' Bronwen said. 'It's Tuesday, Les.' He frowned at her, puzzled. 'I don't usually see you Tuesdays,' she said. 'What's Vera up to? Let you off, has she?'

'I don't need Vera's permission to do anything. I just wanted to see you.'

'Well you're lucky I'm not doing anything special, then, aren't you?'

Leslie smiled and drew her into his arms. 'Any way you look at it, I'm lucky,' he said.

They kissed, slow and gentle. Leslie drew her closer, groaning softly. The door opened and they both jumped. Pete stood there, staring at them. The tableau remained fixed for five more seconds, then Pete turned and walked out again.

'Pete . . .'

Bronwen went after him, but by the time she got outside he had gone.

Later, when she and Leslie had made love, they lay side by side in her big bed, silent, taking occasional sips of wine, savouring their peace. Bronwen thought of these as her golden aftertimes, brief periods when she felt herself in balance, almost carefree.

'God, Bron . . .' Leslie suddenly sat upright. 'I'm getting static off your sheets.'

'Well, if it's giving you ideas, think again, Leslie Parry. It's time you went home.'

He lay with his arm around her shoulder, reluctant to break the contact. An hour had gone unbelievably fast. He felt helpless with time leaking away at such a speed. 'You know, sometimes when I'm away from you,' he said, 'I don't know what I would do without you. You brighten my life, Bronwen.'

He turned on his elbow and kissed her.

'I could have been in your life permanently,' she said, impatient with his sentimental patter. 'But you, you big oaf! I always said she had her eye on you. She had it on any man after her Walter passed away, come to think of it.'

'Now Bron, don't start . . .'

'It's the truth,' she said, laughing softly. 'You remember that dance, first time we met? You'd just joined up.'

'I do.' Leslie clasped his hands behind his head. 'You were a real firecracker. Didn't I ask you to marry me?'

'You did. Me and half the town. I believed you.'

'I know, Leslie said, grinning.

She bit his chest and leapt out of bed. Leslie sat forward and watched her pull on a long T-shirt and sit at the dressing-table.

'It was a good send-off grandad gave me,' he said. 'Good old grandad. I never thought he'd leave me his yard. He hated my Da . . .' His eyes met Bronwen's in the mirror. 'That was a long time ago. If only you'd been around when I came back.'

'If only you'd looked,' she told him, putting a blob of cream on her nose. 'Go on, now, you'd better get back. Bette Davis'll be waiting for you.'

Minutes later, as Leslie got astride his bike across the road from Bronwen's burger wagon, Pete drew up in the old van with LESLIE PARRY: BUILDER on the side. He got out and walked towards the house. Leslie turned the starter a couple of times but the engine didn't catch. Pete stopped and watched for a moment, then came over to the bike. 'You got a problem?'

It was not said with any concern, Leslie noticed. He looked at Pete and saw the resentment. 'You know about bikes, do you?' They held each other's gaze. 'Like you know about plumbing?'

'I know enough,' Pete said, smirking.

'Well let me tell you something – if you want to do a job properly, then you learn it from the ground upwards. Don't cut corners. That said, you did well this afternoon, Pete. Handled yourself well. But you missed two nights last month. You want to get on the new boat, then attend every training session.'

'I was told we were getting an inflatable, a Mickey Mouse . . .'

'There'll be no inflatables in Penrhys,' Leslie snapped.

'They're fast enough though, Les.' Pete was smirking again, still managing to look resentful. 'They're faster than the old lady. I quite fancy myself in one . . .' He mimed a skimming powerboat with his hand. 'Cutting across the water. Some of us lads, well, we don't mind too much.'

Leslie tried the starter again and the engine fired. He revved it gently, looking at Pete. 'Speed don't save lives. Our lifeboat means something, it means you can hold your head up as a proud man.'

Pete nodded towards the house, where Bronwen had come out and stood watching them. 'Is your wife proud of you?'

Leslie restrained an urge to punch Pete in the mouth. 'Don't insult your mother with snide remarks, son. You know why I come here, and so does your mam.'

'So does the whole town!' Pete laughed bitterly and backed away. 'Everybody knows.' He spread his arms. 'I was out of a job, now I work for you.' He turned and headed for the house again. 'It's OK by me,' he called over his shoulder. 'You be my guest, Les. Any night.'

Keeping a rein on his fury, Leslie jammed on his helmet and drove away up the road. As Pete reached the end of the path he almost walked into Bronwen. He side-stepped her and as he passed she swung her arm in a smooth arc and slapped him on the side of the head with her open palm. Pete carried on walking, swinging his shoulders nonchalantly, his left ear ringing like a bell.

3

Later that evening at the George Hotel, George Bibby sat in the bar treating his regulars to an account of the afternoon's exercise on the lifeboat. It was George's talent to enliven any story with extra detail where it was needed, and to get a laugh out of it no matter what. His wife Barbara leaned across the bar, listening, her smile fixed.

'And just like that –' George motioned with spread arms and jerked sideways on his stool, 'the lifeboat rocked, and he was only bloody overboard!' He laughed and his audience laughed with him. 'But we put up a great show, did everything exactly by the book. He came up out of the water with his stop watch ticking.' He lowered his voice confidentially. 'We thought he might have chucked himself in, they've done it before. Les Parry said he was on an exercise once and the DI jumped.'

Steve Bibby appeared while his father was talking. He took a diversion, avoiding the old man's line of vision. At the payphone in the passageway by the bar he tapped in a number, keeping a wary eye on Meryl. After a couple of rings Rufus Myers-Lloyd answered.

'Rufus, it's me.' Steve cupped a hand to the mouthpiece and raised it until his mouth was covered, too.

'How much did you manage?' He nodded, frowning with the effort to hear above the noise from the bar. 'I got another fifty, but I'll get some more. Not yet, I haven't been able to ask him, he's been out, but I'll ask him now, OK?'

He put down the handset and walked along behind the bar. He leaned across and caught George's attention. It wasn't his usual style to be this direct, but time was pressing, and tonight's mission was important. 'Can I borrow your car, Dad?'

George turned from his listeners. His mouth remained smiling but his eyebrows made a frown. 'My car? What for? You're supposed to be studying. Where are you going?'

Steve's face was not built for openness or deception, but he tried hard to look like a straight-as-a-die young man, doing nothing more sinister than acting on a whim. 'Just fancied a drive,' he said.

'Pass your exams, Steve, and I told you, you'll have your own car.' Steve scowled and turned away. 'A minute,' George said, and waited until Steve faced him again. 'I hear that Rufus Myers-Lloyd was in here earlier.' Steve looked away impatiently. 'Now listen to me, Steve. Don't mix with his kind, he's a packet of trouble. Just stay well away, son.'

Steve shuffled off, grim-faced, silently reaffirming what he had believed for a long time, that having George Bibby for a father was the same as having your shoelaces tied together.

'Another round of drinks here, Meryl,' George called.

He grinned at the assembly, failing to notice that as Barbara turned from the till she was minus her rigid smile. Gwilym Davies, due back at the Regal for the second house, put his empty glass on the bar and announced he was leaving.

'What you got showing, Gwilym?' George enquired brightly. 'Not a ruddy Rambo again, I hope.'

Gwilym was about to explain when Barbara leaned forward from behind the bar, blowing a long plume of cigarette smoke. 'I've no interest in the films now,' she said, 'not since it all came out about Rock Hudson.'

She watched Gwilym leave, then beckoned to George. He leaned close, his ear turned towards her. 'There's a lot of money missing from the till . . .'

George stared at her. 'He wouldn't.' He didn't sound convinced. 'What do you want me to do?'

'He's in his room,' Barbara said. 'Just go up later and have a word.'

George found, suddenly, that he could not sustain a bright front. He asked the others to excuse him, he had to attend to something in the cellar.

Up at the manor house, Rufus Myers-Lloyd was lying on the sofa in the sitting-room, his head on one padded arm, feet on the other, watching television. Young James lay on the carpet alongside. The doorbell rang once and Rufus got off the couch with a single jump. He was in the hall and jerking open the door before Steve could ring again.

'Great, you made it.' Rufus ushered Steve in, pushing the door shut. 'Did you get your dad's wheels?'

'Nope.' Steve looked blankly at Rufus, not prepared to get into explanations. 'I steered clear of him. I thumbed a lift from Pete Pugh.'

'Shit!' Rufus looked crushed. He glared at Steve. 'We're supposed to leave at nine. He'll be gone by tomorrow. I've given him a hundred quid up front.'

Steve delved in his pocket. Rufus continued to look destroyed.

'I've got the buyers,' he said, 'everything's set up. He won't give us the cash back, you know.'

Steve pulled out a bunch of keys. 'I got transport,' he said.

The evening was turning grey as Leslie drove along the coast road, taking it easy, letting the breeze refresh him and iron out his mood. Drawing near the lifeboat station he looked down and saw the boathouse door was open. He pulled in and parked the bike at the top of the steps.

Inside Hughie Jones was bent over examining the underside of the boat's hull, shining a halogen lamp along deep grooves in the shiny surface. He jumped as Leslie crept up from behind and goosed him. 'God almighty, you nearly gave me heart failure . . .'

'You're working late.'

Hughie shone the lamp along the gashes in the hull. 'You know we thought we hit something this afternoon? What do you think of that, then?'

Leslie fingered the gouges. Something big and very hard had done that. 'There's nothing on the charts in that area, is there? I didn't miss something?'

'I wanted to show you earlier, but you seemed to have pressing business,' Hughie said, without labouring the innuendo.

'Bron's had trouble with a bit of roofing.'

Hughie nodded. 'Have you got time now? I want you to have a look at the maps with me. It won't take a moment.'

The accumulation of the evening's events – the precious hour with Bronwen, the jarring run-in with Pete, and now this, finding Hughie alone here at the centre of all that gave him purpose – produced a sudden, sweet pain in Leslie, a pang for the fragility of things. He put his arm round Hughie's shoulder. 'I hope it *is* just a rumour about the boat,' he sighed. 'This is my life here, ever since I got out of the Navy . . .'

'Mine too, Les. If they do give us the inflatable, that's me out. Too old.'

They went up to the crew room. Hughie switched on the anglepoise and turned it to a coastal map on the wall. 'Some of these wrecks have been here since before the last war. Look.' Hughie traced a line from Penrhys to an offshore dotted circle. 'September, 1938.' He moved his finger a fraction north. 'That temporary oil-drilling rig's somewhere round here. Blasting, or even a big swell, could shift one of these.'

Leslie peered closer at the map. 'You could be right, Hughie. There must be *something* down there. Oh . . .' Leslie rubbed his hands. 'If we got a wreck it would be a stroke, wouldn't it? We'd have divers, frogmen, tourists, salvage boats – it could mean a lot more work for us!' He laughed, elated now. 'I'll tell you what, Hughie, I'd pay to hire a bloody trawler to drag it close to Penrhys.'

They turned at a noise outside. Through the window they saw Geraint Gower stumping up the stairs towards them, brandishing a sheet of paper. He stormed into the crew room, his face taut with indignation. 'Don't think you can hide up here away from me, Leslie Parry.' He shook the paper under Leslie's nose. 'I am taking my complaints before the Branch Committee. I have *twice* been locked out of the boathouse. That's against the rules. I offered to be boathouse attendant, I'm a responsible man, *and* I'm unemployed –'

Leslie put up a hand to silence him. 'Listen,' he said, 'the reason you didn't get the station attendant's job was because part of his duties is showing visitors around the boathouse, and you are the unfriendliest sod I know!' He put his face close to Geraint's. 'Public relations. You don't even know what it means. Now quit spreading rumours, man, it unsettles everyone.' Leslie went to the door. 'Coming, Hughie?'

'You don't walk off when I'm talking to you, Leslie Parry!' Geraint yelled, following Leslie out.

Hughie rubbed his eyes gently. He heard Leslie yell something – a serious warning by the tone of it – then drive off. Geraint stood outside talking to himself for a minute, then he went away, too. Hughie sighed, glad suddenly to have his solitude back.

Minutes later as Leslie, agitated again, drove past the car park of the George Hotel, Lady Myers-Lloyd was walking from her parked Range Rover to greet a handsome, fortyish man who had just arrived in a Jaguar. They embraced warmly, then linked arms and went into the hotel. In the foyer Barbara Bibby greeted them with a preset smile and fluttering eyelashes. 'Good evening, Lady Myers-Lloyd . . .' With the swiftest glance Barbara ran an inventory of the escort. 'Your table is ready, if you would like to go straight in.'

As the couple entered the restaurant George Bibby came out of the bar. He looked furious.

'Lady Myers-Lloyd just came in with her latest dining companion,' Barbara began, then noticed the look on George's face. 'What's wrong?'

'Steve's not in his room.' With finger and thumb

George smoothed the drooping ends of his ginger moustache. He did that when he was annoyed. 'If he took money out of that till, we both know who put him up to it.' George jerked a thumb at the restaurant. 'I'm going to have a word with her.'

Barbara looked appalled. 'You're not going up to them whilst they're eating?'

George nodded firmly. 'Right first time.'

'But we don't *know* it was Steve.'

'I'm sorry, Barbara, but I'm going to. That boy of hers is nothing but trouble.'

Before going home, Leslie stopped the bike on a high bend of the road that gave him a fine view out across the harbour. In the failing light the sea was dimming to a grey shimmer, with ochre glints from a low cloudy sun. Leslie inhaled deeply, held it, then let it out slow and even, imagining he was exhaling all his tension and turmoil and worry.

He scanned the horizon, seeing the occasional dark blob of a fishing boat, hearing the far-off chug-a-chug of an engine labouring against the tide. Up here, doing nothing more than gauging the wind – it was blowing a civilised 3-going-on-4, from the north – his existence seemed straightforward and measurably pleasant. Nothing much mattered. One of the things he had liked about the Navy had been the nights on watch, the periods when he could be like this, taking stock while nature gave his senses a thorough massage.

He glanced back in the direction of the boathouse, out of sight beyond the cliff edge. For himself and Hughie, and a few others for all he knew, that place held echoes of something holy. Every time Leslie went down the steps and through the door his sense of purpose was at its cleanest and most powerful. If ever he lost that . . .

He turned and looked straight ahead again, coughing to stop himself thinking that way. His mind immediately shot to Bronwen, which promptly made him think of Pete and his holier-than-thou disapproval. The lad's opposition was just the kind of thing that a thoughtful woman like Bronwen might begin taking to heart. Leslie could imagine her coming to him and saying, *Look, I've thought this over, about you and me – it's not an easy decision I've made, but it's for the best* . . .

'Leave it out, for any sake,' he told himself, realising that a quiet mind wasn't on the cards tonight.

The wind began to strengthen and in the space of minutes the sky had grown much darker. He zipped up his jacket and started the engine, pausing to take another long breath of sea air. It occurred to him that his life would be improved hugely, if he could count on peace and quiet at the end of the day, every day, a simple interlude for the good of his battered soul.

'Some bloody hope . . .'

He always went home to Vera. It was crazy, but it was the way things were. He only had one life, he was probably half-way through it, and yet he chose to blight it by shuffling back to the marital home night after night. It contributed nothing to his well-being – it did just the opposite, in fact – and it was not what he wanted. But still he did it.

'So what *do* you want, Leslie?' he demanded, revving the engine in sheer annoyance with himself. 'What are you after?'

He stared at the sea and chewed his lip. *Buggered if I know*, he thought.

He swung the bike back on to the road and accelerated away towards home and duty, remembering what somebody somewhere had said: *The Irish don't know what they want, and they won't be happy until they get it.*

When he stepped into the bedroom ten minutes later, Vera was standing at the foot of the bed in her dressing-gown. The wheelchair was nowhere in sight. She stared reproachfully at Leslie, her hands clasped under her chin. 'Do you know what time it is?' she demanded. 'Did it ever occur to you that I might be worried? That I couldn't sleep?'

'Vera . . .' He pulled off his belt and dropped it on a chair. He put his pager by the bedside. 'I've had a very hard day. I really don't feel like getting into a long drawn-out argument.'

'I don't want to argue, I don't have the strength.'

Vera crawled back under the sheets as Leslie sat on the edge of the bed and began undoing his shoes. She drew the quilt up to her neck. 'Mrs Evans called,' she said. 'Syd Matthews called, too. In fact the phone was ringing so much I had to take it off the hook.'

Leslie stopped half-way through removing a shoe. He swallowed slowly and moistened his tongue. 'Vera, I've told you before, you don't take the phone off the hook.' He stood up, holding the shoe, his face turning red. 'You never take the phone *off the hook*!' He flung the shoe into the corner and turned on her. She was cowering now. 'You can go on at me if it makes you feel any better,' he shouted, 'but don't put other people's lives at risk!'

He strode out of the room, banging the door shut behind him. Vera slid down under the bedclothes until the quilt covered her head. Curled small, trying to get smaller, she whimpered into her cupped hands.

4

The sea wind had shifted and grown colder. By the open wheelhouse of George Bibby's little boat, young James Myers-Lloyd sat huddled in an adult's lifejacket as Steve Bibby steered the boat northwards, a quarter of a mile out from the shore. 'I'm hungry,' James said as Rufus knelt to wrap the jacket more snugly around him. 'And you promised me I could have the hat. It was a deal.'

'It's not my fault you're hungry. You should have eaten your dinner. You're a pain in the butt. What are you? And what are you going to tell Grandma?'

'That it was my idea,' James said. 'I promised, and I am a pain in the butt. You said I could keep it for ever.'

'Right.' Rufus took off the black leather cowboy hat and put it on James's head. 'Because I'll get it in the neck if she comes back and we're not there. So where are we?'

'Listening to Steve's records.'

Steve turned from the wheel at the mention of his name.

'Sorry about this, man,' Rufus said, 'but Hawkeye here has a big mouth.' He held up a warning finger to James. 'You remain glued to that seat. Make one move off it, and I'll smack you so hard. Do you understand me? James?'

'Yes.' The boy nodded solemnly. 'I'm not to move. Can I really – and swear before God – keep Clint's hat? Yes?'

Rufus nodded and flipped the hat down over James's eyes.

It was dark when they finally drew into a tiny cove, its shoreline a rocky strand between the sea and a sloping park dotted with caravans and trailers. Only a few of them had lights on. Rufus told James he wouldn't be long, winked at Steve, then clambered over the edge, wading through the shallow water until he could start hopping from rock to rock. When he reached the edge of the trailer park he turned for a moment and waved.

He made his way through the silent wheeled dwellings to a rusting trailer attached to a beat-up van, parked by a hedge. A dog chained to one of the wheels stood up suddenly, startling Rufus. He leapt back as it began to bark. A curtain in the van was pulled aside, showing a triangle of light. Then the light went out.

Rufus, recovering from his fright, hushed the dog and went to the door. He tapped, waited, tapped again. 'Come on, man,' he said, his face close to the door. 'Open up, it's me.'

There was the sound of a lock being undone, then the door opened. Rufus went in. The only light was above a table, where a red cloth had been used to shade a naked light bulb. Tony, the contact, led the way to the table and indicated that Rufus should sit opposite him.

They faced each other, unsmiling, Tony sombre in his black polo-neck sweater. Rufus tapped the wad in his shirt pocket, the sign of good faith. Tony shook white tablets from a bag on to the table-cloth, then started counting, sliding them aside two at a time. When he had finished and begun scooping them into a plastic bag, Rufus took out his money.

'I gave you a hundred up front and . . .' he counted more on to the table. 'One-eighty. What's the going rate now for each tab?'

'You can get up to a fiver each,' Tony said, 'maybe five-fifty.' He scooped the money towards him and passed over the bag. 'You want anything else? I'm moving on.'

Rufus thought about it.

'Yea or nay?'

'No. Just the tabs.'

As Tony pocketed the money he peeled off one note and laid it aside. From his pocket he took a small folded square of paper and put it in front of him. 'You want a treat?' A humourless smile twisted his mouth for an instant. 'This is special. It would cost you a hundred a gram in London.'

He opened the square, revealing a small mound of white powder. He spread it flat with the edge of a playing card then used the card to chop the powder into lines. 'Try it. It's better than any coke you've ever had.' He rolled the banknote into a tube and passed it to Rufus. 'You don't come down off this for twenty-four hours. Nice and clean. Ice.'

Rufus took the tube and hunched over the powder. So this was ice. Powdered meth. He had never tried it but he had heard the stories. On this stuff, a man could be in knife-edge command of himself and everything around him, and still be as high as Concorde. He put the tube to his right nostril, flattened the left one with his finger, then took up a line with one snort. The tingle was like the shaking of a bell. He looked up at Tony and grinned.

Lady Myers-Lloyd drove along the drive at the manor house, followed by George and Barbara Bibby in their Granada. She parked the Range Rover, got out and marched smartly into the house, the staccato clip-clop of her heels signalling her annoyance. George and Barbara stayed in their car.

In the hall Lady Myers-Lloyd stopped, aware at once that the place was too quiet. 'Rufus? James?'

She went upstairs and found no one. She ran down the stairs again, agitated, banging her arm on the banister as she turned into the hall. 'Rufus! Where are you?'

She went through the sitting-room and into the kitchen. The place was deserted. Back in the hall she tried one more time. 'Rufus? James?'

She stood hearing her echo die, thinking how dinner had been ruined, the whole evening disrupted and the house sale probably torpedoed. She felt herself getting angry.

Outside again she faced George Bibby, who was standing beside his car, ready for a confrontation with Steve and Rufus. 'They're not here,' she said.

George took that in, then turned away abruptly. He opened the car door and got back in beside Barbara. 'Right,' he said. 'I'm calling the police.'

'You took your time!' Steve complained as Rufus clambered back on the boat. 'We're both freezing.'

Rufus smiled benignly and patted his pocket. 'Let's go,' he said. 'I got the goodies.'

Steve started up the engine and turned the boat around, keeping it slow as they nosed their way out among the rocks. As they pulled clear of the cove the wind hit them again, gusting and cold. James, huddled deep inside the lifejacket and under the hat, was scarcely visible.

Ten minutes into the return journey Steve suddenly cut the engine and stood leaning over the side, a hand cupped to his ear.

'What are you doing?' Rufus demanded.

'Ssh! I heard something.'

They both listened. The sound of voices came to them, possibly from up ahead, although the wind was swirling now, making estimates unreliable. Steve thought he detected the faint intermittent purr of a motor, too. They could be hearing the Coastguard.

'I'm not risking it,' Steve said. 'We'll go back into the cove.'

'Eh?' Rufus peered at him in the dark. 'Are you joking? It's a thirty-mile hike by road back to Penrhys.' He stood listening for a minute. 'Come on, there's no one out there. And even if there is, I mean we've got my kid on board, we don't look suspicious. We're just doing a spot of night fishing.'

'What? Without so much as a rod between us?' Steve shook his head. 'No way. We turn back.'

As Steve pressed the starter James came forward, blowing on his hands. 'I'm cold sitting out there,' he told his father.

Rufus turned on him with the over-fast reaction of the chemically stimulated. 'You yelled your head off to come out with us,' he snapped. 'Just sit where I told you to and shut up!'

The engine sputtered to life, turned over a few times, then stopped. Steve pushed the starter again. The same thing happened. After the third attempt he slapped the wheel. 'I think I flooded the engine.'

James, wandering back to his seat in the stern, looked heartbroken. Rufus shrugged. It was a trifling setback, nothing to make a drama about. 'We'll wait ten, twenty minutes or so, give it time to dry out, yeah?'

Steve nodded, wondering if Rufus had been taking anything.

They waited a long fifteen minutes, too cold to say much. They heard no more voices, only the wind and the boat creaking as the waves surged against it. The darkness was infuriating, like an inky cowl blanking out any sense of location or distance. Only the wind direction, cloudy moonlight and winking shore lights gave any clue about their position. Steve began to notice that the lights had grown fewer, and a lot smaller. The sea was choppier now, too.

'That's quarter of an hour,' Rufus announced, peering at the luminous dial on his watch. 'Should be long enough. Start the bloody thing up and get us out of here.'

Steve pressed the starter. The engine turned, coughed, cut out. The second time he tried, it barely turned over.

'I don't know what's wrong.' Steve slapped the wheel again, peering across towards the land. 'Jesus Christ.' The lights were like distant stars now. 'Have you seen how far we've drifted? We're miles out!'

'Anchors aweigh, my boys,' Rufus sang, 'anchors aweigh . . .'

'It's not funny!' Steve yelled.

'You think *I* think it's funny?' Rufus made a wide sweep with his arm. 'This was your idea. *Yours*, not mine. I am freezing cold, hungry, and getting really pissed off. Drop the sodding anchor, or something . . .'

'There isn't one!'

'Oh, great.' Rufus stared up at the black sky. 'What about an oar? Have we got some oars so we can start rowing back?'

James began sniffling. 'I'm cold, Dad,' he called out. 'I'm cold out here.'

Rufus jabbed Steve in the arm. 'Have you got anything at all for an emergency?' he said. 'Like a radio could be useful. Or flares?'

'No way.' Steve hugged himself, shivering. 'No way am I sending up a flare. If my Dad comes out . . . if I get the lifeboat called out he'll kill me . . .'

'Great.' Rufus leaned back on the wheelhouse. 'So in the meantime, what do we do?' He turned to the small, shadowy figure of James in the stern. 'Oi! Keep a look out for pirates!' Turning back to Steve he said, 'Just don't get him scared, OK?'

Steve decided to tinker with the starter, although he knew nothing about it. Rufus went and knelt by James. 'Now listen. You keep as warm as possible. Here.' Rufus took off his jacket. 'Put this round you. And we'll look for the flares, OK? Nothing is going to happen to you.'

A sudden gust took the boat broadside, making it dip violently to port and ship water. James lifted his feet as the flow surged over his trainers. Rufus, still kneeling, felt the icy water seep through his jeans. He pretended it hadn't happened. The engine rattled and sputtered and he looked up hopefully, but it cut again with a clank.

'Flares are supposed to be kept always in a dry box,' James said from the depths of the clothes wrapped round him. 'Grandma says when you light them you have to point them upwards like a rocket, or they go off sideways.'

'You start looking, Jamie,' Rufus said.

James got up, steadying himself on numb legs, then turned and lifted the lid of the bench seat.

Rufus slipped into the tiny forecabin and stood behind Steve, who was on his hands and knees, pointing a torch down into the oily centre of the engine. 'OK, the joke's over now, Steve. I want to send up a flare, we've only got one lifejacket between us.'

'I got them Ru!' James shouted from outside. 'I got them!'

'No!' Steve yelled, pushing himself to his feet, running at James. 'I told you *no*!'

Rufus blocked him, grabbed him hard by the shoulder. Steve was shaking violently, turning hysterical.

'Steve!' Rufus shouted in his face. 'Stop this! Come on, man, straighten out!' Rufus held on tight, a hand on each of Steve's shoulders now. 'OK, blame it all on me, tell your dad it was all my idea, OK? Steve? I'm the bad guy, right? Ex-junkie, so blame it on me. My type don't make heroes.'

The boat lurched again as a squall hit the bows. Jagged waves leapt over the side and splashed across the deck. There was a sudden crack, a *phwoosh* and an upward streamer of light as James released a flare.

'Look! Look!' James shouted as the ball of light crested and spread high above the boat.

'And with one mighty leap he was free!' Rufus roared. '*Yes*!'

At that moment the buoy set loose from the buried

wreck, straining on its tether only feet beneath the surface, struck the underside of the boat, tilting it sharply. Steve and Rufus were hurled to the floor of the cabin. Young James, standing at the side, was thrown backwards into the sea.

'Jamie!' Rufus shouted from the forecabin. 'Jamie! Get down on the deck, lie down!' He pushed himself to his feet, trying to help Steve. 'What happened? Did we run aground?'

The boat surged against the heavy buoy again and the jolt knocked Rufus forward. His face struck the edge of a bunk and blood welled from his nose. On his knees he scrabbled for the torch and found it. He switched it on and crawled outside. The cowboy hat lay on the deck. There was no sign of James.

'Jamie!' Rufus screamed. 'Jamie!' He scanned the water with the torch beam. 'I can't see him!' he howled. 'Shout to me! Jamie, shout to me!'

At the furthest dim reach of the beam of light he saw the orange glow of the lifejacket. There was no saying how far out it was. Rufus charged back to the wheelhouse, blood streaming down his face. He took one end of a coil of rope and tied it to the rail. The other end he tied around his waist, whimpering as his fingers refused to co-ordinate at speed. When he was finally secured he dived over the side, just as Steve let off the second flare.

The water was so cold Rufus nearly passed out. When he was able to breathe properly and the flashing in his eyes cleared he blinked hard and saw the lifejacket eight or ten feet away from him. It was fully afloat, but because it was too big James was sagging down out of it, his face half submerged.

'Jamie . . . Hold on . . .' Panting, gasping, Rufus struggled towards his son, feeling the water drag on his clothes. He reached out with one hand, beating the water with the other, seeing the pallor of the little boy's face as the third flare spread its cold light over the water.

George Bibby drove into the clifftop car park overlooking the lifeboat station and pulled up beside Constable Ernie Hardy, who was standing by the fence, muttering into his radio. George wound down the window. 'Have you found them, Ernie?'

'Not yet.' Ernie tucked the radio into his pocket. He leaned down and put his face to the open car window. 'I'd switch round if I were you, George. I can smell you from here.'

'I told you to let me drive,' Barbara said.

They both got out. A short distance away Lady Myers-Lloyd stood beside her Range Rover. She was staring out at the pounding darkness.

'Old Deckchair spotted an empty mooring,' Ernie said. 'It's your boat, George.'

For a moment George was motionless, registering what Ernie had said, letting it work on him. He went to the fence and looked down over the cliff edge. 'No,' he groaned, the sound barely escaping. 'Surely to God, no. He knows not to, not at night . . .'

Ernie's radio crackled. He took it out, identified himself, then listened with it close against his ear. Barbara clasped George's hand.

'God, Barbara, he wouldn't have taken my boat out, would he?' He turned to her and was seized by a wave of desperate anger. 'I'll bloody kill him!'

He was startled suddenly by the sound of his bleeper and Ernie's. He pushed past Ernie and started to run full tilt down the steps to the boathouse. Ernie, fat as he was, came close behind him.

'Come on!' George shouted. 'It could be my son! Quick, man!'

Ernie caught up with him, grabbed his arm and spun him round. 'No, George,' he panted. 'Not you. You can't be on this one. You just can't, mate. Sorry.'

George tried to complain. Breathlessness and fright closed his throat. He stood there gasping, heartsore, watching Ernie run down to the boathouse.

5

Steve was crying as he leaned over the rail. He felt small again and wide open to harm. More than anything he wanted to be safe, he wanted them all to be safe. He wanted little James to come dog-paddling to the side of the boat and tell him it was all a joke. 'Rufus . . .*Rufus*! Have you got him?'

Wind and water batted Rufus's ears, deafening him. He was ten yards out from the boat, clinging to James, holding his head up out of the water. 'I got you, Jamie, Daddy's got you safe . . .' Rufus sucked in enough air to shout. 'Steve! Pull the rope in!'

For a moment he thought Steve hadn't heard, but then the rope tautened, and as he hugged James close to his chest he felt them being drawn back to the boat. It was slow, and after a minute Rufus realised the weight was too much. With one hand he untied himself and encircled James with the sopping rope. 'Steve! Pull the rope in! Drag it in, never mind me . . .'

James began to move away from him through the water. Rufus swam behind but soon lost sight of the boy. He was a strong swimmer, but he was tired and the cold had numbed him to the point where his arms and legs hardly responded to his need to keep moving.

Steve wound in the rope as fast as he could. In the circling dark he saw the lifejacket get nearer and he began to work faster, his arms aching, the cold clamping him in every muscle. As the boy came nearer the side of the boat, Steve noticed his face was under the water. 'Oh God, oh Jesus . . .'

Steve tugged the rope harder, half aware that the bleached skin of his fingers was tearing on the hemp. 'I'll have you in a second, James, hang on, kid, hang on . . .'

A mile out due north from Penrhys the lifeboat was ploughing against a rising wind. On the bridge, Leslie Parry stared into meaningless darkness and listened on his handset for the Coastguard's radio message.

'Penrhys Lifeboat, Penrhys Lifeboat . . .'

The signal was choppy. At the console David Thomas shifted to the other margin of the wavelength. The signal grew stronger.

'This is Pennant Coastguard, Pennant Coastguard . . .'

'This is Penrhys Lifeboat.'

'Penrhys Lifeboat, further information regarding the flare. Our mobile is on the cliff, now speaking with first informant. The best we can suggest is a bearing of two hundred degrees true from the headland.'

In the wheelhouse it occurred to Leslie that the advice was less than useful. He thumbed the switch and asked David if there was anything on the radar.

'Nothing.'

The searchlight swept the sea and the crew watched from every angle, doing overlapping scans of the water around them. Leslie cursed silently, shielding his eyes, aching to see something. He hated it when they couldn't find the poor souls they were supposed to be saving, hated knowing they were out there in terrible danger with no help on hand.

'*Yess*!' David Thomas yelled suddenly as a blip appeared on the radar. 'I've got something!'

'Take the wheel, Pete!'

Leslie hurried down and took a look. They confirmed the co-ordinates and Leslie called the plot change up to the wheelhouse. 'Hard to port!'

Within five minutes they had George Bibby's boat in the searchlight. Steve was at the rail, waving frantically with both hands. By the time the lifeboat drew alongside he was turning hysterical. 'We've a boy on board!' he yelled. 'He's been in the water! He looks bad! Quick!'

Three of the crew jumped on the boat. While Rufus edged around them, agitated and babbling, they lifted Steve up into the arms of others at the rail of the lifeboat, then picked up James from the deck and passed him across to Leslie.

'That's my son!' Rufus screamed, pulling at his own hair, trying to jump across to the lifeboat. 'My son, that's my Jamie!'

Leslie took the boy to the lifeboat forecabin and laid him on a blanket on the bench seat.

Gwilym Davies was behind Leslie, looking over his shoulder. 'Les? Is he still alive? He was still breathing, but he's blue. His face is terribly blue . . .'

Leslie said nothing. He got ready for the resuscitation procedure, moving fast but taking care to rush nothing.

Gwilym went out again and met Pete leading Rufus and Steve. 'The lad's still unconscious,' Gwilym muttered. 'Get as much information as you can from these two, how long he was in the water, that kind of thing . . .'

Rufus tried to get into the cabin to see James but they led him away, howling. Steve followed, stunned and feeling hollowed out, scarcely aware of himself. He knew he should be feeling pain from his torn hands but there was nothing now, not even the biting cold.

Daylight was bright on the horizon as they headed back for Penrhys. Around the boathouse there was steady activity and an ambulance waited at the top of the steps.

Edward Thorpe stood by the open boathouse doors. Behind him the winch crew prepared for the return of the lifeboat. As they waited, George Bibby appeared. He walked slowly through the boathouse, looking thoroughly wretched. He stood beside Thorpe, staring out at the faint light on the water.

'Is Steve . . .' George cleared his throat. 'He's really all right? You're sure?'

'He's safe, George,' Thorpe said. 'You get back up there to your wife. They'll get the boys off the boat soon now.'

'Thank God, thank God.' Whatever had been holding George together all night suddenly gave way. He struggled to smile through a crumpling face. 'This has been the worst night of my life.'

He turned away to join Barbara, wiping his eyes with his sleeve.

Less than an hour later, when daylight had spread across the cold, cloudy sky, the lifeboat moved in beside the slipway, towing George's little boat behind. Doc Lewis and two ambulance attendants waited for them to tie up.

First off the boat was Steve Bibby, wrapped in a blanket, sobbing, half-way in shock. Rufus sat on a bench seat, still behaving oddly, as if he had found himself in a completely alien scenario.

'Barry,' Leslie called, 'will you get Rufus ashore?'

Barry Mitchell came forward, putting out a comforting arm. 'Come on now, Rufus, there's nothing you can do, we best get you away from here. Come on, son.'

Rufus got up and walked a few steps, then he stopped suddenly and began to resist. He clutched the leather cowboy hat and waved it from side to side. 'I want to see James!' He was agitated, eyes darting about, looking for his son. 'Why won't you let me see him?'

Leslie loomed up, blocking his forward movement. 'Just go with Barry, son. There's nothing you can do.'

Frowning, shaking his head, Rufus stumbled as Barry pulled him away. They got as far as the rail when Rufus decided this was not what he wanted to do. He began struggling. 'He's my boy,' he said, his voice jerky, trembling. 'He's my son, and he'll want his hat. I want to give him his hat, all right?'

Doc Lewis stepped forward and put his hand firmly on Rufus's shoulder. 'Go to your mother, then go to the ambulance. She needs you, she's been waiting for you. There's nothing you can do, we're all here now.'

Rufus seemed to consider the command, deciding whether it was valid or not. After a moment of frowning and pulling the blanket about himself, he went with Barry up to where his mother waited.

When they had moved away Leslie passed over the small body of James, wrapped in a red blanket. An ambulance attendant placed him gently on a stretcher on the ramp.

Doc Lewis stepped forward and pushed aside a

corner of the blanket. He put his finger on the thin, cold neck where the carotid pulse should have been, pressing gently. He glanced at Hughie who was standing nearby and shook his head. An attendant drew the blanket over the child's head.

Steve Bibby was ahead of Rufus as he reached the top of the steps, trying to tell his tearful parents how sorry he was. Rufus turned to his mother. She stared at him, her face wracked with the strain of fear and worry and anger. Rufus wet his lips. 'It was all my fault,' he said. 'They didn't understand me, I had a right to be with him, give him his hat . . .'

When his mother made no move towards him, Rufus let Barry lead him away to the ambulance.

Lady Myers-Lloyd saw Doc Lewis come to the top of the steps. He was followed by the two ambulance attendants carrying the stretcher with the body of James, wrapped in the blanket. Hughie walked alongside.

'Where is James?' Lady Myers-Lloyd asked the doctor. 'Where is he, please?'

Doc Lewis touched her shoulder gently. 'I am so sorry,' he said.

She looked at the small shape on the stretcher and a terrible howl escaped her. 'James! Oh, dear God, James . . .' She bent over the stretcher, touching the lifeless child's hair, the grief like a knife in her heart.

Later, as Leslie walked up the ramp to the boathouse, he heard Pete Pugh behind him, talking to Gwilym Davies. 'Barry was saying that if we'd had a fast inflatable, one stationed at the harbour, we could have got there faster –'

'Cut it out,' Gwilym hissed, shoving Pete. 'Now's not the time.'

'That's what it's all about though, isn't it?' Pete insisted. 'Bloody timing.'

Leslie stopped walking suddenly and turned. Pete and Gwilym nearly walked into him.

'You know, do you?' Leslie said, glaring at Pete.

'I'm just saying what you're always banging on at me about,' Pete said.

'Oh yes. So you tell me – what factors are vital in a search? Come on, know-all, tell me.'

Pete backed off.

'What about you?' Leslie turned to Gwilym. 'Come on then, you tell me what factors are most important in a search.'

Gwilym frowned for a moment, then his face cleared. 'Visibility and, er . . .'

'And?'

'Accurate bearings?'

'Correct,' Leslie said. He turned to Pete. 'How long do you think it would have taken to sweep that area for that little boat? Given that we had poor visibility, and on the bearings the Coastguard gave us – how long?'

'All I was saying was, we would have got there faster –'

'Bollocks! We would have been there all bloody night and not found it. It was the radar that picked it up.'

Pete stiffened defensively. 'It doesn't matter now though, does it?' he said. 'Little James still didn't make it.'

'No, he didn't, Leslie said. 'But you tell me what Mickey Mouse inflatable that you know carries radar equipment. Go on . . .' Angrily he punched Pete on the shoulder. 'Tell me then!'

Pete and Gwilym backed off and went around him, walking away. Hughie stepped forward and patted Leslie's arm, trying to soothe him. 'I know how you feel, Les, it's the same for all of us.'

'No it's not.' Leslie's voice was husky now, on the verge of tears. 'He died in my arms. So small, but I couldn't make him breathe.'

He turned away from Hughie and walked slowly back to the boathouse.

6

On the day of James Myers-Lloyd's funeral the minister spoke of the sea being a mighty force that demanded our respect. He said it was an element of frequent tragedy, and that when a tragedy occurs at sea, or on land, we learn the hardest lesson of all, that a life lost will never be returned. From that awful event, he said, from the pain and grief it caused, human beings gain an understanding of the eternal workings of divine providence.

If the occasion had not been so profoundly sad, if it had not induced such a pressure of stricken silence, there were people at the graveside who would have argued with the minister. There were fishermen, lifeboat-men and the widows of both, people with scarred and disfigured spirits who could have said no, there is no understanding, the pain causes only bewilderment and isolation and a deep, dark suspicion that no loving God would permit such a calamity.

As men sang the twenty-third psalm in Welsh, turbulent emotions churned behind stolid faces. The sheer obscenity of a child's death forced tears from people who had come determined not to cry. Down in the harbour a wreath of white lilies was placed on the water and allowed to drift out to sea.

Days later the remnants of the wreath still bobbed near the outer sweep of the harbour. Life went on, encouraging memory to fade. Experts came and examined the mysterious marks on the underside of the lifeboat and on George Bibby's little boat, too. Others took preliminary soundings in the approximate area where the damage occurred. Not long afterwards, a mile and a half to the north of Penrhys and a mile out from the shore, four huge buoys with flashing lights appeared, marking the wide perimeter of the sunken wreck. Beyond them a Trinity House tender began taking sonar soundings to establish clearance for vessels operating in the vicinity.

Shortly after nine o'clock on the morning after the buoys appeared, a diver suddenly surfaced beside one of them. He pressed himself close to its side, making his presence scarcely noticeable; from a short distance he was no more than a shadow on one side of the buoy. As the water settled around him he took the regulator from his mouth and spat.

'Steady now, Alex,' he muttered to himself, slipping off his mask. 'Take your time . . .'

He breathed with his mouth wide open, turning his head slowly either way, taking his bearings. He moved gently around the buoy until he was on the other side, with a full view of the other three buoys and the tender. He stayed there for a long time, simply looking.

Up on the cliffs, flat on their bellies, Leslie and Hughie took turns at watching the tender through heavy binoculars. They did not see the diver.

'They're testing for a clearance depth but they won't let any diver near,' Hughie said, the binoculars clamped to his eyes. 'Not until it's been decided to move the wreck, or disperse it.'

Leslie sat up and unscrewed the top of his flask. 'How long will all this take, then?'

'It could be weeks, months even. It'll depend on how old the wreck is. And nobody can touch it, not until Trinity House find out who the owners are.'

Leslie swallowed some coffee and took the binoculars again. The presence of the wreck excited him. He took no trouble to conceal that. 'What do you think it is then, Hughie? It's a good size if those markers are anything to go by . . .'

'No salvage firm can get a look in yet, that's for certain.' Hughie stood up and shaded his eyes, blinking at the dazzle from the water. 'And that means nobody can take anything from the wreck without permission. They've got to make an application to the Receiver of Wrecks. They'll decide if finders can keep anything they come across.'

'Uhuh.' Leslie stood up. He punched Hughie's arm. 'We found it though, didn't we?'

They walked back towards the old builder's van. A thin breeze blowing up from the sea brought the sudden, clear putt-putt of an outboard motor. Leslie and Hughie looked at each other, then went back to the cliff edge. A small black inflatable with an outboard motor was heading out towards the marker buoys.

Leslie raised the binoculars and focused. 'It's Geraint! Now what the hell is he up to?' He looked at Hughie. 'Didn't you see him?'

Hughie shook his head, keeping it casual, wanting no discussion of what he could and could not see. 'He's just nosing around, you know him.'

'Well . . .' Leslie frowned at the hunched, distant figure of Geraint Gower. 'Anybody putting in a claim

– we're first. There could be a lot of money tied up in that wreck.'

They walked back to the van.

'Salvagers will be lining up after it, Les,' Hughie said. 'You and me have got no equipment.'

Leslie opened the van door. 'If it's worth big money, Hughie, we'll hire what we need. That's *our* wreck.'

They got in the van and drove off. Leslie dropped Hughie at the lifeboat station and went straight to the yard.

When he got there, Pete was loading bags of cement on to an open-backed lorry. 'What time do you call this, Les?'

There was no response, beyond Les getting out of the van and slamming the door. Pete wondered if he had miscalculated his tone and made the joke sound like a criticism. Ever since the little showdown between them at the lifeboat station, Pete was keen to raise their relationship to a sufferable level, if no higher.

'We've been viewing the wreck,' Leslie said, coming across. 'Hughie thinks they might blow it up.'

'He'd know, would he?'

Pete was sure he had got the tone right this time. He had meant to imply Hughie knew nothing about much. To get off the topic he spread his hands and looked up at the clear blue sky. 'We should get cracking, Les. If this weather keeps up we can finish George's car park.'

Leslie's enthusiasm was obviously elsewhere. He scratched the tip of his nose thoughtfully. 'We still got those old diving mags?'

'I think they're in the toilet.'

'Great.' Leslie moved off across the yard. 'I'll be right with you.'

Pete stared after him, feeling a tickle of exasperation.

Out on the sea, fifty yards from the nearest marker, Geraint Gower cut his outboard motor and sat back, fingering his beard, staring at the buoys and the tender. It was so quiet, so incredibly still, that he could hear the ping of the sonar. From a bag beside him he took a bunch of folded charts, opened them and spread them across his knees. For several minutes he studied them intently, following his moving finger with narrowed eyes. Then he studied the buoys again, through binoculars this time.

The interior of the bank had been selectively modernised with new booths and tables and comfortable chairs, and an annoying rope barrier for customers to queue beside. The old counter and the metal scrollwork above the anti-gas screens had been retained as a gesture to the past. One cashier was on duty at her till, the other two did obscure things behind CLOSED signs.

In the area in front of the barrier, at one of the shiny new tables, George Bibby sat with his bank books and paying-in slips and a big bag of change, looking as he usually did when he came to conduct hotel business with the bank. Beside him stood Thorpe with his rolled umbrella and the folded pink baton of the *FT* under his arm, looking as if it had been his own decision to pause on the way to the door marked MANAGER: PRIVATE. In fact George was trying to get Thorpe interested in a proposition, and Thorpe, detained against his will, was hoping for a gap long enough to let him slip away and put the matter well behind him. None of this was lost on the cashier, Doris, who appeared, as usual, to have noticed nothing in particular.

'Now I know charts of the seabed are updated,' George said, struggling to stop his excitement pushing his voice up a note or two. 'It's done for all sorts of reasons, but it doesn't automatically follow that the whole area is surveyed. So what I've been thinking is, that wreck could have been moving gradually over a number of years, right?' He tapped the table to focus Thorpe's attention. 'I am right, aren't I?'

'I suppose so,' Thorpe said, 'but I doubt if it'll be anything of value. Probably be an old fishing vessel.' He looked pointedly at his watch, then nodded to the cashier. 'Can you buzz me in, Doris?'

He started to move away.

'No, wait . . .' George got up and came after him. 'I'm serious.' He decided to jump in with both feet. 'I wanted to discuss the cost of backing a salvage operation.'

Thorpe paused. His face went into its noncommittal mode.

'Have you got a minute?' George said, with a hint of pleading. 'It won't take long at all.'

The office door buzzed open. Thorpe held it with his arm and nodded George inside. 'You should have made an appointment you know . . .'

Further down the town, outside the police station, Inspector Barry Mitchell was leaning on the open door of the police car, talking to Leslie Parry, who had slipped away from the job at the George to buy a paper. He had spotted Barry and decided to check on the current legal position regarding the wreck. As he listened to Barry he absently twisted a diving magazine between his hands.

'We're not letting anyone down in the water around there just yet, Les. It's a safety precaution.' Barry was treading the fine line between official cop-speak and friendly chat, something he had to do rather a lot in Penrhys. 'You seen this morning's paper? David Thomas is doing his usual. The idiot's said it could be a Spanish galleon.'

Leslie's mouth opened by itself. 'It isn't, is it?'

'No way.' Barry got into the car. 'I'll see you later.'

As Leslie walked off Barry stuck his head out of the car. 'Les! The hot water!'

'Oh, yeah . . .' Leslie turned, nodded. 'It's in the books, Barry.'

When Leslie got back to the hotel, Pete was standing in the kitchen doorway taking a mug of tea from Meryl. Leslie handed Meryl his copy of the local paper. 'I see that boyfriend of yours has been trying for a scoop again.' He poked his head into the kitchen. 'George in, at all?'

Meryl wasn't listening. She was too anxious to clear up a point. 'It's not serious, me and David . . .'

She looked hard at Pete to make sure he had caught that. It was difficult to tell whether he had or not. He was gulping his way to the bottom of the tea mug. When it was empty he handed it back. 'Your brothers have got a salvage yard, haven't they?' he said. 'Is there money in it, then? Salvage?'

'A few years back,' Meryl said, following Pete to the mound of cement at the side of the car park, 'when me Dada was alive, they got some wood, just crates, and they made a fortune with them, antique pine, all the rage now. I know they only got two, but they were selling them for months.' She stepped closer to Pete, lowering her voice. 'They were getting a carpenter mate to knock them out, and then they would dump them in the sea for a few days, and then clean them up again.'

Pete turned the cement with a shovel, his face expressionless, non-judgmental. 'We all got to make a living,' he said, then paused, looking around. 'Well, maybe not all of us – what's that Les doing?'

There was no sign of Leslie. Pete shook his head as if he were the boss and Leslie the hired help. He pointed to a coiled hose attached to a standpipe and asked Meryl to turn it on. She crossed daintily to the pipe and did a calculated bend-over to pick up the hose, showing Pete her white panties under the edge of her miniskirt. She turned on the tap and spun to face him, giggling, letting him have a momentary blast from the hose. Big dark wet spots appeared on Pete's shirt.

'I wouldn't do that!' he warned her, laughing.

Meryl stepped closer and sprayed him again. Pete planted the spade in the cement and made a grab for the hose. He caught it and turned it on Meryl, spraying her. As they cavorted and laughed, a severely battered truck stopped outside the entrance to the car park. The back was piled with broken sinks and old cookers. The driver, Tom Taylor, banged on the horn.

'Talk of the devil,' Meryl said, going across.

She leaned into the truck, displaying her legs again for Pete's benefit. He swallowed hard and carried on shovelling cement. 'What do you want?' she asked her brother.

'I'm picking up Mitch, he's coming in from Swansea. You'd better get some food in for tonight.'

Tom was younger than Meryl, though he struggled

always to exhibit a gritty maturity. He would have been handsome if his eyes had not been so pink-edged, if his skin had been better and his mop of dark hair washed and cut in some coherent shape. His filthy overalls were oddly harmonious with the rest of him.

'Will Mitch be staying?' Meryl asked.

'Yeah.' Tom looked past her. 'You heard anything about that wreck?'

'No. Have you found out who owns it?'

'No. But Trinity House issued a local notice. Nobody can do anything. We're just taking a look, so keep your mouth shut. See you later.'

Meryl stepped back and Tom drove off. As she turned she caught Pete watching her. She smiled warmly, hedging her bets as always.

By lunchtime Geraint Gower was back home, sitting at the kitchen table with a notebook and pencil beside him, thumbing through Yellow Pages. He picked up the telephone and began tapping in a number as his wife Dilys came in through the back door with a bag of groceries. She put down the bag, unbuttoned her coat and wandered out to the hall.

Geraint pressed the handset closer to his ear as someone answered. He coughed before he introduced himself.

'The name's Geraint Gower,' he said brightly. 'I called earlier. Ah, good, now did your assistant tell you what I was calling about?' He listened, his expression darkening a shade. 'Oh, well. Sorry to have bothered you.' He put down the receiver. 'Cheap bugger.'

Dilys came in from the hall, still wearing her coat. She was a once-pretty woman, still young but ageing visibly. 'I thought you were meant to be at the manor doing the garden,' she said.

'Lady Myers-Lloyd is in Bermuda, Dil. She's hardly going to care which day I cut the grass, is she?'

'Poor love,' Dilys said, peering into her bag of groceries. 'I don't think she'll ever get over losing James. Steve's gone away, too. Barbara's sent him to his gran's.'

'Dil, I'm working,' Geraint muttered, comparing a number in Yellow Pages to one in his notebook.

'Running up a telephone bill, more like.'

'Well.' He glared at her. 'You got any better ideas how I can get the equipment? Have you?'

Dilys set about unpacking the groceries, banging the items into the cupboards. 'Even if you do get it on trial,' she said, 'where are you going to practise?'

Geraint's face darkened for the second time in as many minutes. 'Why do you do this, Dilys? Anything I come up with, you've got to put it down.'

'It'll be you going down, Ger, and probably get yourself into trouble.'

He stared at her indignantly. 'I'm not stupid enough to attempt it without knowing what I'm doing, woman. I was a clearance diver in the Navy.'

'That's news to me.' Dilys glanced at him sidelong. 'Any road, I don't know why I'm getting bothered. You've not even got a pair of flippers, never mind a wet suit.'

'*Fins*, Dilys, you don't call them flippers. And I might just get everything I need, and for free. Then you'll laugh on the other side of your face.'

'I'm not laughing, Ger.' Dilys turned to him, her eyes warm suddenly. 'Far from it. You know I've always gone along with everything, but this is crazy, and I would have thought, with you being on the lifeboat crew –'

Geraint slapped his hand flat on the table. 'That wreck could make us a fortune! If I get the contract they'll all look like bloody fools, because it'll be mine. *All mine.* I'm going to get it before any other bastard.'

'Listen to you,' Dilys sighed. 'You're talking as if the whole town's against you.'

Geraint sat back in his chair, nodding. 'Maybe they are, Dilys. Nobody ever gave me a break. I've got nobody but myself.'

'You've got me. And the kids.' Dilys leaned close and looked at him. 'I just worry . . .'

Geraint stood up and put his arms around her. He drew her close. 'Don't,' he said. 'Just don't worry, and I'll prove I'm worth standing by. I've got to try it, Dil, I hate going down the DSS.'

Dilys kissed his cheek and stepped back. 'I'll go and get the kids.'

As she left Geraint sat down and ran his hands through his hair. 'Ah, Dilys, Dilys . . .'

He wished, so often, that he had the words to tell her about the fire in him, the burning drive to succeed, in spite of the cards he had been dealt. He knew he could be a thundering success, all he had to do was make himself available to the main chance.

He stared at the table, goading himself, imagining what it would be like to get the edge on all the others and leave them choking on his dust. His mouth tightened. Taking a deep breath he snatched up the handset and began dialling the second number in his notebook.

7

Hughie was in the crew room at the lifeboat station with charts spread out before him on the table. He chewed a sandwich as he studied old records of the waters around Penrhys. Deckchair was sweeping up, creating small puffs of dust as he delivered one of the deathless tales that he had threatened to write down in a book one day. Mercifully, Hughie thought, this one was finally arriving at the payoff.

'So I looked at the bones,' Deckchair said, 'they weren't small enough for a rat, and I looked at the eight black round pebbles . . . it was all done up in a parcel, see. Guess what it was?'

'You've got me, Deck,' Hughie said, still examining the charts. 'I have no idea.'

'The bones of a ship's cat!' Deckchair said triumphantly. He paused in his sweeping to explain. 'See, in the old days, every sailing ship had a cat on board to catch the rats and mice . . .'

'Ah!' Hughie leaned really close to a chart and jabbed his finger on the intersection of two lines. '1942, another one sank, so if my calculations are right . . .'

He crossed to the map on the wall, peered at it and nodded. 'Well,' he said, 'David Thomas was talking through his fat backside again. That's no sailing ship; I reckon it's one of these three.'

Deckchair came and looked at the careful notations of wrecks on the map. His interest in them was marginal, at best. 'When a sailing ship looked like it was heading for disaster,' he said, 'first thing they did, they put the cat in a bag with eight pebbles. You know why?'

'No,' Hughie sighed, 'but I have a feeling you're going to tell me.'

'Because they thought that the sea would be satisfied with the nine lives of the cat, and wouldn't take a member of the crew. That's what they done in the old days. Superstitious, see . . .'

Hughie rubbed his eyes for a moment, then stood drumming his fingers on the map. 'Really, you know, that wreck's got to be one of these boats, Deck.'

'Or it could be an old 'un, not on the charts,' Deckchair suggested darkly, prodding the map. 'The bones was found there, 1930s. Mind you, a dead cat's not the weight of a ship, is it?'

As Hughie was gathering up the charts Geraint Gower walked in. He looked suspiciously amiable. He asked Deckchair if he could have a private word.

'Was that you out by the marker buoys this morning, Geraint?' Hughie asked him.

Geraint whipped round, surly, glaring. *That* was more like him, Hughie thought. 'No it bloody wasn't me!'

'Good,' Hughie nodded, 'because it's nasty currents out that way, even more so with that wreck, and a small outboard motor's not going to tackle a sudden swell.'

'I've been around these waters here since I was a kid,' Geraint blustered. He cocked his head at Hughie. 'What were you doing there?'

'Just taking a stroll,' Hughie said, going to the door. 'I'll be in the boathouse, Deck, if anyone wants me.'

'Right, Hughie.' Deckchair turned to Geraint. 'Do you know what I found once, back in the 1930s?'

'Listen, Deckchair –'

'Eight black pebbles and –'

'Deckchair, I want you to do something for me,' Geraint said. 'I'm expecting some equipment . . .' He tapped the side of his nose. 'It's from an old mate in the Navy, he runs a diving school now. Anyway, the stuff'll be addressed to the lifeboat station, but it'll say G. Gower's Aqua Club.' He took a five pound note from his trouser pocket and showed it to Deckchair. 'I want you to call me as soon as it's arrived.'

'I've got a deep-sea diver's suit, Geraint. Bought in an auction, it was. It's immaculate.'

Geraint did not show a flicker of interest. He pocketed his fiver and made for the door. 'You call me, Deck, and there's a few quid in it.' He paused, touching the side of his nose again. 'Just between you and me, understand?'

Deckchair nodded. With nobody left to talk to he began sweeping again, whistling tunelessly to himself.

Throughout the day the Trinity House tender continued to drag its heavy iron bar back and forward, working to a grid, taking soundings. From a sheltered gap in the cliffs the diver, Alex, watched the activity. Dressed in a navy sweater and jeans now, he smoked one cigarette after another as he watched through binoculars. He was stamping on the butt of his eighth Benson and Hedges when an electronic chirruping issued from a worn hold-all at his feet. He reached in, took out a mobile telephone and unfolded it.

'Yeah?' He listened, his eyes still fixed on the tender. 'No problem. I'm going back down later, I want to take some photos. See you around tennish.'

He closed the phone, slipped it back in the holdall and put the binoculars beside it. He walked to an old Post Office van parked nearby and opened the back doors. His comprehensive and immaculate diving gear was laid out inside, ready for use. He dropped the hold-all inside, shut the doors and turned, taking another hard look at the tender.

Going to the driving side he saw two men walking across the coarse grass away from the cliff edge. They were about three hundred yards away and not likely to see him. Even so, Alex got behind the wheel smartly and started up. They didn't look round as he pulled on to the road and drove off.

They were preoccupied. The shorter man was Griffith Taylor, Meryl's older brother. He was square-faced and light-haired, though not as fair as Meryl, and he walked with the rolling gait of a man habituated to heavy physical work. The other man was Mitch Morgan, tall and wiry, with dark good looks that failed to conceal a thuggish streak.

'It's a big bastard all right,' Mitch said, looking back over his shoulder. 'Look how far apart the friggin' markers are.'

'And no divers allowed near the place,' Griffith said. 'There's not even been a sniff of this.' He glanced to the left and stopped. 'Hang on . . .' He watched a vehicle disappearing along the road, throwing up dust. 'It's OK,' he said. 'Post van.'

'When this gets out,' Mitch said, 'you'll have divers going off those cliffs like lemmings. But that's no galleon. A frigate, maybe . . .'

'They're still trying to find out who might have owned it. Have you heard anything from that insurance bloke?'

'No, they've got no particulars yet.' Mitch started rolling a cigarette, in spite of the breeze. 'I think we better take a look. First come, first served. If it's tasty we put in an application to the receivers before anyone else. We'll go down at first light.'

A few minutes later Hughie was walking by the harbour, carrying a fresh coil of hawser from the chandler, when he saw Griffith and Mitch get out of a green Jaguar. They went up the gang plank of a flaking old fishing boat tied up among the smart yachts and speedboats.

'Hello, Griff,' Hughie called, 'how are you keeping?'

This, Hughie would freely admit, was the busybody in him coming to the fore. He had an endless curiosity about people and what they were up to, especially when he came across any of them bending harbour rules, which was quite often.

Griffith stopped. Mitch continued on up to the deck.

'I'm doing all right,' Griffith said. 'How are you?'

'Can't complain.' The pleasantries over, Hughie got to the point. 'You'll get it from the Harbour Master, you know. Has your friend got the OK to anchor there?'

'He's not stopping,' Griffith said.

Before Hughie could prolong the encounter Griffith turned and followed Mitch up on to the deck. They went down into the cabin and watched through the porthole as Hughie walked back the way he had come, heading for the Harbour Master's hut.

'That's the trouble with this town,' Griffith muttered. 'Interfering buggers.'

The static air in the cabin was dense with the smell of oil and festering seaweed. Mitch pulled a bottle of scotch from under a pile of dirty diving gear and unscrewed the cap. He took a couple of hard swallows as they watched Hughie talking to the Harbour Master, pointing towards the boat.

'Everybody pokes their noses in.' Griffith tutted softly. 'It'd be best if you moved out and got anchored as near the wreck as possible.' He looked at Mitch. 'Fancy a spot of fishing, do you?'

'Depends on the catch,' Mitch said as they went back up on deck. 'It's been a while since I had a rod in my hands.' He leered, demonstrating that his features were well suited to it. 'How's your Meryl, then?'

'Leave her alone, Mitch,' Griffith said sharply. 'I mean it. No need for bad feeling between us.'

'Just a polite enquiry,' Mitch assured him. He slapped Griffith on the shoulder. 'Go on, hop it, I want to sort all the gear out.'

As Griffith went down the plank he said he would see Mitch later. Back in the cabin Mitch drank another inch from the whisky bottle, watching Griffith drive off. Turning then, he made himself face the dirty diving equipment. He groaned and took another quick snort from the bottle.

Late that afternoon Leslie Parry came clumping into the station hut, pulling off his overalls. He had come at the earnest request of Hughie, who entered the hut behind him. 'What's all the urgency?'

'Meryl's brother was down at the harbour,' Hughie said. 'Guess who was with him in an old fishing boat that didn't have permission to be there?'

'Who?'

'Mitch Morgan.'

'I thought he was still in the nick.'

'Scuppers us, doesn't it?' Hughie said.

Morgan's adroitness as a deep-sea scavenger was well known. A robbery from a sunken Admiralty cruiser had won him his recent jail stretch.

'Not if we get in before him.'

'Oh yeah?' Hughie made an old-fashioned face. 'How are we going to do that? We've not got any gear. Forget it.'

'I'm working on it,' Leslie promised him. 'We might have to take on an extra partner, mind you . . .'

Meryl pushed a ladle round and round a big pot of stew, keeping her head well back to avoid getting the meaty smell in her hair. She was at the cooker in the cluttered kitchen at home, a room that was well beyond the stage of being simply untidy. The kitchen door led directly to the yard, where her brothers kept some of their scrap. There had been an inevitable overspill, with rusty castings, coils of rope, canisters, fragments of diving equipment and bulky metal abstractions littering the kitchen floor and stacked against one wall. Things had been that way for so long Meryl hardly noticed now, and the muddle never hampered her when she cooked or served meals.

The table, on the other side of the kitchen from the

cooker and the sink, was set with cutlery and plates for three. Tom sat in an old ruptured easy chair, looking at charts. At home he was a comparatively passive soul, preferring to save his *machismo* for the outside world where a man had to keep on proving himself, even when he didn't feel like it.

'I've made sandwiches, and there's fruit and flasks of tea and coffee,' Meryl said. 'I'll have to go to work soon.'

Tom paid no attention. Being ignored by her brothers was something else Meryl was used to. She went to the window. Griffith was coming through the gate with Mitch.

'How long will he be staying?' Meryl asked.

'No idea.' Tom looked up. 'Got any beer, have we?'

Meryl brought a clutch of bottles from the fridge. As she put them on the table Griffith came in. Mitch was at his back, leering already. It occurred to Meryl that he probably thought he was playing the handsome devil. He took off his donkey jacket, put it on the back of a chair and stayed by the door, leaning on the wall. He began hand-rolling a cigarette, trying to emanate a measure of cool.

'That smells good Meryl,' he said.

'It's just stew,' she told him. 'If you want to sit down I'll serve it up.'

The exchange was awkward for her. She did not want to look directly at Mitch; at the same time, she didn't want her brothers to think she was being rude. She had the impression that for the time being, it was important not to offend Mitch. 'The bottle opener's on the side table,' she said, noticing that in spite of the invitation to be seated, Mitch was still leaning by the door.

'How are you, Meryl?' he drawled. 'You've put on a bit of weight since I last saw you.'

'So have you,' she said, wishing at once that she hadn't said it, since any response was likely to encourage him. She turned to her brothers. 'Shall I serve it up or not? I've got to go to work.'

She expected no answer and she got none.

'They're still dragging the wreck,' Griffith told Tom. 'We reckon it must be lying very deep. If it had been a masted ship they'd have started breaking it off.'

He went to the table, rubbing his hands, trying to drum up some enthusiasm for the meal. He also tried to grab more of Mitch's attention. 'I told you it'd be some kind of tanker, didn't I?'

Mitch was obviously more interested in Meryl. He took the open bottle Tom handed him and drank from it, keeping his eyes on the girl as she ladled the stew into bowls.

'I don't fancy going out at night, Mitch,' Griffith said.

'Nor will anybody else.' Mitch smiled at Meryl. 'I'm hungry.'

Meryl blushed, but she still didn't look at him.

All three men finally sat at the table. Meryl brought the bowls from the cooker. As she put Mitch's in front of him he slipped his arm around her waist. 'You got a young man then, Meryl?'

'Yeah,' Griffith said, 'she's got that pratt from the *Reporter*.'

'He's not my boyfriend,' Meryl said, swiping Mitch's hand away.

'Ahh . . .' Mitch put on his version of a gleeful face. 'That means you're free then, does it?' He patted his knee. 'Come and sit down.'

Griffith watched, annoyed, as Mitch tugged at Meryl until she was sitting on one of his knees.

'I've got to go to work,' she said, her face crimson.

Being inclined to a carefully graded approach where women were concerned, Griffith could never understand some men's driving need to behave like rutting stags the minute they got near young females. It added to his annoyance that his little sister, for all her protestations, probably liked that kind of approach. He tapped the table impatiently, determined to stick to business. 'How much is this caper going to set us back then, Mitch?'

'Cost of the boat,' Mitch said, stroking Meryl's hip, 'the equipment, and we split the profits fifty-fifty.'

Griffith nodded, but he couldn't ignore Mitch's behaviour any longer. His anger erupted, and it was directed at his distressed sister. 'That skirt's too short!' he barked. 'You'll give Mitch the wrong idea, especially since he's been inside for five years. Go on, get out!'

Meryl leapt off Mitch's knee and strode out into the hallway. Mitch watched her leave, then smiled coldly across the table. 'It's only fifty-fifty, Griff son, because no way am I going down on my todd. It's too dangerous, you see. It's a two-man dive.'

8

The cardboard crate measured five feet by three, and it was bound with stout nylon tape. It stood just inside the doorway at the lifeboat station and when Geraint arrived Deckchair was leaning on it, waiting for him.

'My God . . .' Geraint looked surprised. 'I didn't think it'd be so big. Have you got a cart?'

'Well . . .' Deckchair scratched his cheek, thinking. 'There's the one I use to stack the deckchairs, but that's down on the beach.'

'There's a fiver in it.'

Geraint rubbed his forefinger and thumb together to sweeten the inducement, but Deckchair felt he should be difficult about this. Being awkward was an old man's privilege, and it was one he didn't abuse half often enough.

'What's in this crate, then?' he demanded. 'The label says Penrhys Lifeboat Aqua School.'

'Just get your cart, Deck. Go on.'

Deckchair's stubbornness fled as fast as it had come. He wasn't good at being awkward and a fiver was a fiver, after all. He ambled off. Geraint took a pair of pliers from his pocket and began attacking the binding. His breath squeaked in his throat as he struggled with the tape, and he began to sweat with anticipation.

'Come on, come on,' he panted as the pliers chewed

the tape instead of cutting it. '*Come on!*' He pulled, twisted and jerked, using both hands. 'Ah! There . . .' The tape gave with a satisfying *snap*! 'That's more like it . . .'

He pulled off one length and started on another, aware that his hands were sweaty too, slipping on the pliers. Doc Lewis had warned him about letting this happen, so had Dilys. He was inclined, when he got excited, to gallop ahead of his ability, that was how the doctor explained it to him. Dilys said he fizzled and sparked like a dodgy microwave.

He paused and steadied himself, taking deep, slow breaths. There was nothing wrong with him, he knew that, he just got worked up about some things because he had a powerful imagination, he could think ahead a lot clearer than most folk. Once, getting a prescription for his sinuses, he had sneaked a look at his notes when Doc Lewis left the room to take a phone call; he had memorised a sentence scrawled under the printed heading GENERAL OBSERVATIONS. It said:

> *Patient demonstrates excessive and unrealistic responses to trivial and occasionally imagined pressures.*

Cheeky sod, Geraint had thought. Lewis was a good doctor, he would allow him that, but he didn't have the perception to realise Geraint Gower was a man of exceptional alertness, a man who could spot trouble coming when others felt no hint of it, a man who knew when people had decided to gang up on him, no matter how they denied it or tried to keep it a secret.

He cut off two lengths of tape and managed to pry open a flap of the crate a few inches. The gear was neatly packed in thick transparent polythene with an enticing brand-new smell. He knew he should wait until he had the stuff away from the lifeboat station before he started examining it, but he couldn't help himself, he had to see. He started pulling off the plastic adhesive tape, but Deckchair was back with the cart before he got beyond the first layer of polythene.

Between them they heaved the crate on to the cart and managed to bump it up on to the road. Since the only way to Geraint's house was uphill and the gear in the crate was a dead weight, he coaxed Deckchair to help him push it home. 'There'll be an extra fiver in it for you,' he promised.

It was hot, strenuous work, and half-way to the house Deckchair said his spine was threatening to pack up. A hundred yards further on, when they were both panting desperately, Deckchair said he was getting distinct pains across his chest.

'Just stop moaning and push, Deck!'

The old man stood away from the cart and wiped his forehead with his sleeve. He put up both hands, indicating he was through. 'I've got to get back for me dinner,' he said. 'Mam'll be worried stiff.'

'Well bugger off then,' Geraint yelped at him, his eyes bulging. 'I'll manage on my own.'

'But it's my cart, I might need it.'

'You'll have it back, nobody's going to want a deck-chair at this time of day, are they?'

'What about my ten quid?'

That ended the dialogue. Geraint put his shoulder behind the crate, gripped the handles of the cart, grunted ferociously and got it moving. He staggered on up the road, his breath whining. Deckchair watched him for a minute, then turned and started walking the other way.

At that moment, on the clifftop overlooking the marker buoys, Leslie Parry, George Bibby and Hughie Jones were standing side by side, arms folded, watching the shimmer of evening light dance on the water.

'I had a word with Edward Thorpe this morning,' George said, making a clean breast of his commitment thus far. 'He said he'd look into the costs of financing a salvage operation, but you know him – unless he had it authorised by the Duke of Edinburgh he wouldn't risk lending me a cent.'

'We could all pool in a few quid,' Leslie said.

George nodded, but he looked pained. The notion of reckless expenditure sent queasy pangs across his stomach. 'Is there some way we could get a sneak look?' he said, glancing at Leslie, then at Hughie. 'Sort of as insurance before we laid out any cash, like.'

'No way,' Hughie said flatly. 'Thorpe won't even think about doing anything that would harm Penrhys's chances of getting the big boat.' Hughie unfolded his arms and stuck his hands in his pockets. He'd had enough of this. 'I'm going back up to the boathouse.'

'What's the matter with you?' Leslie said.

'I work there. All right?'

Hughie strode away across the rough grass.

'Well.' Leslie shrugged. 'Me and you, George. Come on.'

Back at the lifeboat station Leslie and George studied the charts in the orange-red sunlight slanting through the windows. Hughie sat apart, huffily drinking a mug of tea, shaking his head from time to time.

'We'll take my boat,' Leslie said, 'crack of dawn,

get as close as we can to the markers, and have a look . . .'

'And then what?' Hughie chipped in. 'You won't be able to see anything, you'll just be wasting your time.'

'I've bee working on that,' Leslie said, doing a slow-motion wink. 'See . . .' He pointed for George's benefit, 'if we drop anchor here, and we get a deep-sea diving kit –'

'What?' George stepped back. 'Where the hell are you going to get one of those things from? That's for starters. And then who are you going to get to go down?'

'We hire the bloke,' Leslie said, his voice calm and reasonable. 'That's what I've been checking into. We'll hire somebody to go down for us.'

George thought about that. 'What about Geraint?' He saw he had lost Leslie's sympathy, instantly, at the mention of the name. 'He's done some diving, hasn't he? When he was in the Navy? Les?'

'He's not coming anywhere near this caper,' Leslie said. 'Geraint Gower is a bloody liability.' He fumbled in his pocket and pulled out a slip of paper, peering at his handwriting. 'North Sea Salvage Company. We'll try them first, and there's three others.'

George was getting uneasy again. He looked at Hughie, then back at Leslie.

'If Edward Thorpe got to hear about this . . .' Hughie muttered, letting his voice tail away ominously.

'Hughie . . .' Leslie took a tight hold on his patience. 'If we get that inflatable and you're out of a job, mate, this could be your future. Besides, Thorpe's got no involvement with it, we're using my boat.'

'I'm not having anything to do with this,' Hughie

said, putting down his mug. 'I'm sorry, but that's the way I feel. You're on your own, Les.'

Leslie put away the charts, then he and George left, exchanging gruff good-nights with Hughie. He watched them go, then sat letting the silence gather around him.

This is no good, he told himself after ten minutes.

He stood up and stared through the window at the dying light. For a moment it felt as if there was no one else but him left on the planet. It was a feeling that had gripped him a few times lately. The loneliness of a person cut off from his family is a special and bone-deep kind, it is an emphasis of what is, set achingly against what was. Hughie decided he should make himself busy, since self-pity disgusted him.

He decided to polish a few brass fittings. He dug out the Brasso, shook the tin and realised it was empty. Being fastidious about supplies, he knew there would be a new tin in the stock cupboard on the other side of the boathouse. Half-way across he stopped, frightened. He put his hands over his eyes, then slowly took them away. He turned his head, looking from side to side, breathing shakily.

On the way to the telephone he walked into a chair. He gripped the back of it, forcing himself not to panic. When he felt steadier he picked up the receiver and tapped out a number. Doc Lewis answered.

'Is that you, Frank? It's me, Hughie. You got surgery tomorrow morning? No, no, nothing urgent, but I'd like to see you. Fine, I'll be there.'

He put down the phone and tried to remember what he had been doing.

Brasso.

He went to the cupboard again, more slowly this time, almost warily, wetting his lips and trying to whistle.

Out on the coast road, riding his bike back to the yard, Leslie saw Deckchair hobbling along ahead of him. The old man was weaving about on the side of the road with his thumb stuck out. Leslie drew up beside him. Deckchair looked very glad he had done that. He also looked worn out.

'Give us a ride back home, Les, I'm knackered.'

Leslie told him he would come a cropper wandering about the road like that. 'What have you been up to?'

'Les, listen . . .' Deckchair leaned close, ignoring the question. 'Is the lifeboat starting an aqua club?'

Leslie stared at him, misunderstanding. 'Who have you been talking to?'

'Mam's been on at me to get rid of it,' Deckchair said. 'It takes up a lot of space, see.'

To Leslie, this sounded like delirium. The old man was known to ramble at times, although until now Leslie had believed it was all down to how hard you were prepared to listen.

'I've got it out in the shed, it's in perfect condition.'

Leslie started the bike again.

'Used to be a lot of salvage companies, going back a few years,' Deckchair said, raising his voice over the noise.

Leslie revved the engine, preparing to leave.

'Must be worth a few quid. Got the ropes, the wheel and everything. Give us a lift, eh?'

'You need a helmet.'

'Got that an' all,' Deckchair shouted. 'Huge thing, like on them space suits.'

Leslie let the throttle die back. 'Deck . . .' His eyes were wide as he leaned towards the old man. 'You've not got a deep-sea diver's outfit, have you?'

The gardens around the manor house were ornamental in the loosest sense, conforming to a series of patterns, but none of them so tight or so severely husbanded that nature had been kept entirely in check. In the evening light they had a misty look, the diversity of colours blending into each other with no clear margins. Red, yellow, blue and pink flowers, muted now, looked daubed, like touches from a paintbrush.

The house was silent, locked up, the owner and her son gone separate ways with their grief. Birds that Lady Myers-Lloyd had fed in the evenings still came to wait on the lawn, the grass a little longer each time they landed. Tonight there were more than a dozen of them, pecking the ground, moving in tiny circles, as if they wanted no one to know they were waiting.

They scattered as Geraint Gower came down the lawn in full diving gear. He looked like a vast black frog with the gift of walking upright. He stopped by the edge of the swimming pool and uttered a heartfelt curse. The tarpaulin was tightly battened down, covering the entire surface.

He forced himself to stay calm. This was just another challenge, he decided, and a small one, compared to the trouble he'd had getting into the wet suit and the boots and the buoyancy jacket. It was all worth it, he had learned a few things – and besides, no achievement was worthwhile if it came too easily.

He sat down and spread the spiral-bound manual on thc ground. Dividing his attention between the book and the equipment, he made himself familiar with the parts of the regulator, then checked it was emitting air properly by letting it blow against his face. When he was sure it was completely in order he put it carefully in his mouth, pulled the mask down over his face, and closed his eyes, trying to imagine he was under water.

He could not convince himself.

Opening his eyes, he pulled the regulator from his mouth and set about struggling with the tarpaulin. It took a couple of minutes to unhook one end. He raised it and looked into the water. It was green and murky, a lot like a cess pit.

Geraint cursed again, scaring a few more birds. Fortune had a way of resisting him, he thought, but on the other hand, he could view all this as a test of his determination. Sludge and slime or no, he was going to have a bit of practice in there.

For half an hour he bobbed and swam in the pool, testing every piece of the equipment, getting himself used to its curious feel and the way he could adjust his buoyancy and his depth. It was not the most comfortable experience, but nobody had told him it would be. As time passed he came to the conclusion that, for somebody with his natural aptitude, using this tackle out in the sea would be a doddle.

He surfaced and checked the contents gauge. Hardly any air had been used, so he decided he would have another ten minutes in the pool. He noted the time on his watch, then submerged.

He had been in the pool for a total of forty minutes when Barry Mitchell, on duty at the police station, received a report that the gates at the manor house had been opened. Ernie Hardy was just taking off his cycle clips when Barry passed the message to him.

'Go over and have a look, will you, Ernie? It might be local kids off the estate. Best to check, anyway.'

Ernie put his clips on again.

'I'll be on the desk if you need back-up,' Barry called. 'Just radio in.'

Ernie said something quiet and insubordinate, and went back to his bicycle.

Geraint, meanwhile, had decided his training was over. He got out of the pool, eased the regulator from his mouth, and stood for a minute to let the water and algae run off him. Then he took off the mask and set about putting the tarpaulin back over the pool. It was hard work, but he kept reminding himself that was all to the good, it was battle practice.

When he had covered the pool he picked up the manual between finger and thumb and waddled around the side of the house to where he had left his bag. He dropped the manual inside, went to the garage and opened the doors. The Range Rover was inside. He felt along the shelf at the side and found the keys behind an old Golden Syrup tin.

Five minutes later, as Constable Ernie Hardy pedalled up the lane, he heard the roar of an engine ahead and had to swerve to avoid the Range Rover coming towards him. He tried to see the driver, but the figure behind the wheel appeared to be sheathed in black, including his head.

Barry wobbled to a standstill as the Range Rover

swept on past. He watched it disappear, throwing up a trail of dust. It occurred to him that he should call the station.

9

Leslie came banging into the kitchen with his helmet and leathers still on. His sister-in-law Phyllis was fussing by the oven. She turned and smiled nervously at him.

'How does steak and kidney pie sound?'

She held one plate piled high with food for Leslie and one with a child-size portion for herself. Leslie had often wondered, though silently, how she managed to get so generously upholstered when she ate so little.

'Lovely.' He eased off his helmet and put it on the side. 'Where's Her Majesty, then?'

'Watching TV.' Phyllis nodded at the wall. 'I'm making up a tray for her, she's a bit poorly today.' She glanced at Leslie quickly, gauging his mood. 'Erm, did she mention to you that I'll be in the box room? It's just until I find a little place. Lady Myers-Lloyd has gone abroad, and then, with James gone . . .' The simple mention of the child made Phyllis's voice tremble. She cleared her throat. 'She won't need me, you see, and I'd nowhere else . . .'

Leslie nodded, pulling off his leathers. 'Stay as long as you like, Phyllis, you're always welcome.' He held up a finger. 'On condition you don't apologise for breathing.'

'Thank you.'

She finished heaping mashed potatoes and peas

around the hummock of pie on Vera's plate. She picked up the tray and Leslie opened the door for her. 'Could you take my cases up the stairs?' she said, going into the hallway. 'It's a bit difficult to get past the chair lift.'

Leslie was staring at Vera's plate. 'Bit poorly, you say? It's not affected her appetite, then . . .'

Phyllis hurried off to the lounge, smothering a giggle.

Vera did not rouse herself that evening until 'News at Ten' came on. When she finally opened the door and came into the hall, she walked as if the effort were draining away every last ounce of her strength.

She stopped and stared. Leslie was on his knees at the foot of the stairs with a screwdriver. Phyllis was sitting in the lift as it came slowly down.

'Go back up again, Phyllis,' Leslie told her.

She turned the switch. The chair stopped, shuddered, then began to ascend. Phyllis giggled. Vera swept dramatically to the foot of the stairs and supported herself with a hand on the wall. 'Phyllis! What are you doing?'

'I'm trying to get it so it doesn't stick,' Leslie told her.

'I think you should take it out,' Vera said coldly. 'It's a hazard, like everything else you bring back. And it's not worked, anyway, since you took all the bathroom appliances up and down in it.'

Leslie pushed himself to his feet. 'I only put it in to help you.'

'You put it in, Leslie, because you get it for nothing. Still, my disabilities have never been a priority.' Vera glared up the stairwell at her sister. 'Get out of it, Phyllis. I want to go to bed.'

Phyllis turned the switch again and came slowly to the bottom. She stood up. 'It's very safe, dear,' she assured Vera. 'We've taken all my suitcases up in it.'

The telephone rang. Leslie grabbed it. 'Leslie Parry speaking. Hello, Pete.' He frowned, listening, then his face cleared. 'You've got it? Great! Contact Gwilym. I'll see you in the morning.'

'Good news?' Phyllis said, as Vera scowled.

Leslie nodded, and permitted himself the exuberance of clapping his hands together. Hard.

Later, as Vera lay in bed, putting Post-It stickers on occasional pages of a magazine she was leafing through, Leslie came into the bedroom, winding his alarm clock. Vera looked up. She was about to say something when there was a distant rumbling of plumbing, followed by the rhythmic beat of pumping water. Phyllis emitted a squeal, then a muffled titter.

'She's switched on the Jacuzzi,' Vera said.

They stared at the wall for a moment. Leslie laughed. 'I bet she's not had this much excitement for twenty years.'

He went to the door and listened. Vera made a disapproving mouth. She flipped through her magazine, trying to ignore the sound of the water and her sister's girlish laughter.

'She's having a ball in there,' Leslie said, moving away from the door.

'I hope for her sake the ceiling can take the weight of all that water.'

Leslie started to pull off his sweater. He paused with it half-way over his head. 'Is your Phyllis still a virgin, do you think?'

Vera's mouth now did what Leslie called its impersonation of a cat's arse. 'Are you sleeping in here tonight?' she demanded.

Leslie nodded, pulling off his sweater and dropping it on a chair. 'I'm not getting a bad back on that sofa, and Phyllis is in the only other decent bed. Sorry to inconvenience you.'

He sat down heavily on the foot of the bed to take off his shoes and socks. Vera winced, clutched her magazine and edged over to her side of the bed.

Geraint had driven Lady Myers-Lloyd's Range Rover as far as the narrow slip path leading to the lower coast road. He slowed down and stopped as the headlights picked up a row of cones and yellow markers and a sign prohibiting access.

He got out, looked about him, then moved the cones, clearing a path. He got back in the cab and drove on, keeping the headlights dipped. On the lower coast road he drove slowly, watching for the shale path the locals used to short-cut their way to the harbour's edge. When he saw it he slowed the engine even more, crunching softly on the shale and straightening out on to the sharp incline.

At the landing stage he got out, carrying his fins and his buoyancy jacket with the air tank attached. In the dim, dying light he put on the gear and clambered down off the stage where his inflatable was tethered. For a moment the vessel swayed dangerously. He balanced himself in the middle, his hands clutching the sides.

When it settled he undid the rope tethering the boat to the landing stage and pushed off. He began to drift as he tried to start the outboard motor. It sputtered lifelessly. After three tries his temper was near flashpoint. He stopped and made himself sit still until the pounding in his ears died down. Then he tried again, and the engine started.

He aimed himself in the direction of the winking buoys, a good long distance away, seemingly further at night than during the day. Holding the short tiller with one hand he slid the other under a plastic sheet beside him. For reassurance he ran his hand over the items covered by the sheet: a spare can of fuel, a torch, blankets, flares, ropes.

'A professional always comes prepared,' he muttered, secure in the certainty that he was every inch the professional, whatever anybody else said.

The sea was turning choppy and the wind began to rise. He scarcely felt the cold through the wet suit, but he could feel it on his face and on his hands, the chill and the spray, bringing unwelcome thoughts of lonely peril and souls lost to the waves.

The lights of the buoys rose and fell but seemed to come no nearer. Geraint hunched lower, cutting his wind resistance, willing the boat to go faster. The wind and the wet and the time it would take – they were all part of the same thing, he reminded himself. They were all components of adversity, and nothing was achieved without adversity. He made himself bare his teeth at the night as his mind ran the same phrase over and over, his talisman against the frightening dark:

I am the master of my fate, I am the captain of my soul . . .

On her old bike, her skirt hitched high as ever, Meryl Taylor pedalled back home from the George, taking her time, enjoying the clear night. She swung the bike from one side of the road to the other, singing the chorus of a Lisa Stansfield number, la-la-ing the bits she didn't know. Looking up suddenly she saw Pete Pugh in front of her, walking his old sheep dog.

'Well, well . . .' She braked and slid off the saddle, landing expertly with her feet spread. 'Isn't this an amazing coincidence.'

Pete wasn't sure what she meant. 'I always walk this way,' he said, 'taking Rudy for a late piss. I'm surprised we've not crossed paths before.'

'Crossed paths!' Meryl echoed him extravagantly. 'Like star-crossed lovers that, isn't it?'

'Not quite.' Pete made to move past her. 'I'll see you again, no doubt,' he mumbled. 'Good-night.'

Meryl put a hand on his arm. 'Walk my way and we can talk,' she said. 'I'd like to get to know you better, Pete.'

He stared at her a moment, scarcely making out her features in the dim light. He shrugged. 'All right,' he said.

They walked along the road together, the dog foraging ahead. To his relief, Pete had no need to make conversation. Meryl launched into a monologue that was loosely her life story, with occasional anecdotes that took her down sidetracks that had nothing to do with her history. After ten minutes she had told Pete most of it, and by the time she brought the narrative up to date she was sitting on the saddle with one arm around his shoulder while he pushed the bike along the road.

'When Dad died, they all looked after me. They got ever so protective, especially Griff. He's old now, thirty-odd, but he still treats me like I was a kid.'

A car rounded the bend behind them and drew

up. It was the police panda. Barry Mitchell wound down the window. He asked if either of them had seen Geraint Gower. Pete said he hadn't laid eyes on him.

'He didn't come in the George,' Meryl said. 'Have you tried the Working Club? He sometimes plays darts in there, and the beer's cheaper.'

Barry thanked them and drove off, waving. They walked on in silence, Meryl leaning closer now, letting her weight sag on Pete's shoulder, her breath fanning his cheek. At her gate she got off the bike and stood close to him, closer than he found comfortable.

'Good-night then,' she breathed. 'Thanks for walking all this way.'

Pete swallowed audibly. 'Good-night,' he croaked.

Meryl didn't move. She put her head closer to his. He caught the aroma of her scented skin, stronger now they were motionless and facing each other.

'You can give me a friendly kiss good-night if you want, Pete.'

There was a short silence. The only sound was Rudy snuffling by the wall.

'Better not,' Pete said. 'David is a mate of mine, so no point in starting something up. I've been trying to tell you, I like you a lot Meryl –'

She tried to interrupt.

'No,' he said, 'listen, I know you said it's not serious between you and him, but maybe you should tell David that, and not string him along. That's what I wanted to tell you.'

Another silence, then Meryl laughed softly. 'I just meant a friendly good-night kiss, Pete, not a tongue-down-the-throat job.'

He leaned forward to kiss her on the cheek. He was an inch away when she turned, pressing her half-open lips on his, forcing his mouth open. Her breasts thrust forward, making a warm imprint on his shirt. She stepped back sharply. 'Sorry,' she said, her voice throaty. 'Good-night then, Pete.'

His trousers felt incredibly tight and warm. He turned away, disconcerted, speechless.

Meryl slipped into the house by the back door, easing it shut. She tiptoed across the kitchen in the dark, hands outstretched in front of her. She was nearly at the door to the hall when somebody grabbed her from behind. Strong arms round her waist pulled her back. She smelt sweat and stale breath. Mitch.

'You're a sexy little thing, aren't you?' He nuzzled her, raking his stubble across her cheek. 'I've been watching you out there with your boyfriend. Really pouting and flirting, weren't you? Eh?'

Meryl tried to break away but he drew her closer, his stinking breath hot on her face. 'Come on, lighten up, baby . . .'

'You better let me go, Mitch,' she panted. 'I'll scream. My brothers won't like it, they'll come and get you.'

His arms tightened sharply, hurting her. Suddenly it was serious. This was violent. Meryl struggled harder, hearing anger in the way he grunted, feeling it in the bruising grip of his hands.

'You can scream all you want!' he hissed. 'It's just you and me, so how about giving me what you give your bloke?' He tried to turn her to face him. 'Come on, Meryl . . .'

He forced her head round and tried to kiss her on

the mouth. She butted his nose. He gasped and caught her by the hair. 'Don't make me slap you around!'

He pulled her close again, slobbering on her face. His fingers hooked in the top of her dress, tearing it. Meryl pulled back with all her strength, giving herself space. She brought her knee up hard into his groin.

'Aah! Jesus!'

Mitch doubled over, letting her go. She raced to the back door, jerked it open and ran out into the night. Mitch groaned, clutching himself, hearing footsteps in the hallway. He kicked the door shut and rolled on to the couch.

The hall door opened and the light came on. Tom was standing there, blinking. 'Mitch? What's going on?'

'Cramp,' Mitch grunted, mashing his face in the cushions. 'I got terrible cramp . . .'

Griffith came lumbering in. He looked at the clock. 'Meryl's still out, is she?' His brother nodded. 'I'll give that boyfriend of hers a good slapping next time I see him.' Griffith leaned over the couch and looked at Mitch. He was still writhing and groaning. 'Get him something for his hangover. It's time we were moving.'

Meryl kept running until she was at Pete Pugh's house. She stopped by the garden gate, gasping for breath. She could see Pete in a lighted window upstairs. She picked up a pebble and threw it without aiming. It hit the glass with a sound like a small gun going off. Pete spun, stared at the window for a second, then opened it. He leaned out into the dark, trying to identify the shape by the gate.

'Let me in Pete, please,' Meryl whined, her voice small but clear as a bell. '*Please*, it's not what you think.'

'Go away, Meryl.' He sounded martyred.

'Something happened to me! Please let me come in, I'm freezing out here.'

Pete stayed at the window a moment longer, then he closed it and moved away. Meryl ran up to the front door and stood there, hugging herself for warmth. The door opened. Pete looked terribly unsure of himself. He was trying to look stern and responsible.

'Oh, thank goodness!' Meryl stepped into the hallway. 'It was that Mitch. He tried it on with me, Pete. It was terrible . . .'

Pete looked at her for a moment, picturing it. Galvanised suddenly, he put his arms around her. She hugged him tightly, pressing her cold lips to his neck.

10

Geraint sat gingerly on the side of the boat, adjusting the mask on his face, breathing air through the regulator. He glanced over his shoulder, making sure the anchor and buoy marker were secure, then he flipped over backwards into the water. A moment later he surfaced, fumbled along the edge of the boat and reached inside for his torch.

As he descended, the beam of thin light stretching ahead of him, he felt the cold penetrate his suit, numbing skin and muscle. For what seemed like minutes there was no sign of anything solid, only his own bubbles streaming past his eyes and the torchlight beaming off into the foggy depths. He began to wonder if the big marker buoys could have been put in the wrong place, or if the wreck had drifted.

Then suddenly he was looking at it. It was huge, a misty, ragged-shaped hulk only a shade darker than its surroundings, but it was real, there was no way to mistake its solidity.

Geraint swam closer, directing the torch beam right and left, seeing portholes and tangled rails and riveted steel plates. A swirling current drew him down and sideways, giving him a panicky moment until he righted again and found himself beside a length of chain stretching off into the gloom. He followed it, gripping its rusted length until he came to an opening in the side of the wreck. He hesitated.

Faint heart ne'er won fair lady, he sternly reminded himself; *nor anything else, for that matter . . .*

He swam through the opening and found himself in a cabin. Shining the torch around he saw another opening, a doorway with the door lying alongside, its hinges rusted away. Moving through the gap he saw another door straight ahead. It was shut tight and covered in slime and flaking rust.

He tried pushing against the door but it was rigid. He braced his feet against a post and tried again. He only succeeded in making the blood pound in his head and stars dance in front of his eyes. Veering away from the door he dropped the torch. It somersaulted down through the churning silt beneath him. He bent to pick it up and was aware of something large and dark floating above him. He grasped the torch and shone it upwards.

His heart jolted and he nearly dropped the torch again. Right in front of him, floating horizontally, was another man in a diving suit. This was Alex, the professional diver, although Geraint did not know that. He did know Alex was dead, however. His waxy face was set in the last horrible rictus of suffocation, the severed end of the air line drifting behind him, one final glassy air bubble trapped on its lip.

The next two minutes were a blur of colliding impulses, until Geraint found himself rising at speed through the water. He surfaced by his boat, shaking violently, floundering in panic. He clambered in, pulled off his mask and spat out the regulator.

'Oh my God . . .' Grunting, fumbling, he tried to start the motor with freezing hands. 'Oh my dear God . . .'

Minutes later, prowling along the lower coast road in the panda, Barry Mitchell spotted Lady Myers-Lloyd's Range Rover near the landing stage. He parked the panda and went across to have a look.

The Range Rover wasn't locked. He opened the door wide and shone his torch inside. Clothing, clearly identifiable as Geraint Gower's, was piled on the front passenger seat. Barry went back to the panda and reached in for the radio. Then he paused, hearing the *putt-putt* of an outboard. He walked back to the landing stage and peered out at the dark water. The sound came nearer, but he could see nothing.

He went back to the panda, got in and turned it around to face the sea. He switched the headlights on full beam and got out again. Standing at the edge of the landing stage he saw something; it was oddly detached, moving sharply from side to side. After a minute he realised it was a hand, and near the hand was another light blob, a face. It was a man in a black diving suit, he realised, and whoever it was, he looked very agitated.

The inflatable drew in to the side and the engine died. The man in the wet suit and fins clambered up on to the stage. Barry watched him warily, moving back towards the panda, his hand outstretched ready to grab the radio.

'It's *me*, Barry. It's Geraint.'

Barry straightened, tightened his jaw. He stepped forward again. 'What the hell do you think you're playing at?' he demanded. 'This is a restricted area.'

Geraint didn't appear to be listening. He pulled the mask over his head and pointed out across the dark water. 'You'd better get the police out here, Barry.'

'And what do you think *I* am?'

'There's a body.'

'What?'

'A dead body. Out there in the wreck.'

'Are you sure?'

'Of course I'm bloody sure!' Geraint yelped. 'I just came eyeball to eyeball with it!'

As Barry and Geraint got into the panda, a rowing boat was making its way out to the spot where Mitch Morgan had anchored his old fishing boat. Griffith Taylor and his brother Tom did the rowing while Mitch sat in the stern, huddled in the folds of his overcoat. The night air, coupled with the lack of sleep, the throb in his groin and the queasy aftermath of too much whisky, had made him as sick as he believed he could get without actually passing away.

'One of you'll have to come down with me,' he said. 'I feel terrible.'

'It'll have to be Griff,' Tom said. 'I've not dived before. Griff?'

The rowing boat slewed round alongside the fishing boat. Griff took hold of the ropes dangling over the side and pulled himself to his feet. 'Let's just get the hell out of here first, shall we?' he snapped. 'We don't want anyone to sight us. There'll be fishing boats out at this time.'

It was ten past three by Leslie's watch as he stood jabbing the doorbell on Bronwen Pugh's front door. A window above him opened. Pete stuck his head out and said he would be right down. He slammed the window shut again and a second later the door opened. Bronwen stood there in her quilted dressing-gown.

'Go ahead, Leslie Parry,' she said, 'wake the entire household. Do you know what time it is?'

Pete came down the stairs carrying his wellington boots.

Bronwen asked Leslie if he wanted a flask of tea.

'No, Phyllis made me one.' He looked at his watch and then at Pete struggling into his coat. 'Come on, lad, the others'll be waiting.'

Bronwen wanted to know where they were going at this hour.

'It's business, Bron.'

'Don't you go getting my Pete into any trouble now, Les.'

Leslie turned and walked back along the path. As Pete followed him Bronwen took a grip on his arm.

'What's going on?' she said.

'Like Les said, Mum, it's a bit of business and we want an early start.'

'I didn't mean that.' Bronwen pointed upstairs. 'What's going on?'

'Nothing's going on.' Pete glared at her indignantly. 'I'll see you later. Don't you go nosing in my room.'

Bronwen closed the door behind him and went through to the kitchen. A moment later Meryl came down the stairs, tiptoeing, carrying her shoes. She got to the front door and turned the catch silently.

'There's a pot of tea on in here, Meryl love,' Bronwen called.

Meryl froze. She turned just as Bronwen appeared at the kitchen door.

'No need to go rushing off,' Bronwen said brightly, standing aside, beckoning her in. 'Nothing's urgent at this time of the morning, is it?'

In less time than she would have believed, Meryl Taylor found herself relaxing with her elbows on the table, sipping tea in the homely clutter of Bronwen Pugh's kitchen. The transition from embarrassed intruder to comfortable visitor had been accomplished seamlessly and entirely without pain. Bronwen had not pressed for an explanation and Meryl had not volunteered one. Instead they had a relaxed conversation and, as happened so often, Meryl found herself doing most of the talking.

She sat now with her hands around a warm cup, telling Bronwen roughly the same story she had delivered to her son a few hours earlier. 'I was just seventeen when she died, just after I won Miss Penrhys. Oh, she was proud. I suppose in a way it was Mum's dream, mine too. But you know what they say, success too early . . .'

'Yes, love,' Bronwen said, smiling, 'but it makes it all the sweeter second time round.'

'Aw, I don't think I'll win it again,' Meryl said, missing the point. 'I didn't even get to the final six last year.' She hesitated, then said, 'Has Pete got a girl?'

'Maybe,' Bronwen drew her fingers across Meryl's torn shirt. 'He didn't do that, did he?'

'No, no, he never touched me.' Bronwen thought she caught a trace of disappointment. 'He slept on the floor.' Meryl took a final swallow and put down her cup. 'I'd best go home. My brothers will have a fit.'

They went out to the hallway together. 'You know, Meryl love, if you ever need to talk, woman to woman like, I'm always here.'

'Thank you very much, Mrs Pugh,' Meryl beamed.
'And it's not Mrs. I never married anyone.'
'I know,' Meryl said, 'I was just being polite.'
Bronwen roared with laughter.

Over at the police station Geraint Gower, gaunt and sunken eyed, was leaning on the counter with a blanket draped around his shoulders, looking like a figure from Welsh mythology. Barry Mitchell, telephone in hand, was flushed with the exertion of venting his feelings. He had just finished telling Geraint, in a number of colourful ways, how much of an outright pest and bloody nuisance he was.

'You don't need to shout,' Geraint said petulantly. 'And what's the point of calling out the lifeboat? The bloke was dead.'

'I've only got your word for it, Geraint Gower, and we don't know if there's any more.'

'There was just one!' Geraint threw up his hands, almost losing his blanket. 'His air line was sliced in two, I told you. The edges of the cabin were sharp. If I hadn't got professional training, I could have done the same thing.'

'You shouldn't have been down there in the first place. Plus you had Lady Myers-Lloyd's Range Rover.'

'She said I could borrow it.' Geraint started pacing the length of the counter. 'I've been doing her gardening. Phone Bermuda if you don't believe me.'

Barry wasn't listening. He had tapped a number into the phone and now it had been answered. 'Hughie, I'm sorry to wake you. I've been told there's a body down in the wreck.'

Geraint stopped pacing and stared. 'What are you

calling him for? All we've got to do is go back. I'll go down again, and –'

'Just shut it, Geraint.' Barry listened to Hughie. 'I'll be right over.'

'What's going on?' Geraint's eyes were wide, his nostrils flaring, sensing a new conspiracy. 'What did he say?'

Barry called through to the back of the station for Constable Ernie Hardy. There was no response. He called again. 'Ernie? *Ernie!*' Barry shook his head. 'This whole town's going mad.'

Then Ernie appeared. He looked confused and befuddled. He was never at his best during the night hours.

'Get down to the coast road,' Barry told him, 'and you let nobody, I mean nobody, near the shore.'

'What's happened?' Geraint demanded, the image of a wild-eyed prophet in his blanket. 'What did Hughie say?'

Barry glanced at him. 'You're not the only maniac after that wreck.'

Suddenly Geraint looked possessed. He raised one trembling, accusatory finger and stabbed it into thin air. 'I know who it is!' he cried. 'It's that Irish bugger, isn't it?'

'Who are you talking about?'

'Bloody Les Parry, he's the maniac.'

A few seconds after 3.45 a.m. Leslie's old van drew up in the harbour. Leslie and Pete got out and opened the rear doors. George Bibby and Gwilym Davies unfolded themselves from the back and stood stamping their feet, restoring the circulation. With the help of Leslie and Pete they eased a huge wooden crate out of the van and carried it all the way down to the slipway steps. They set it down carefully and stood catching their breath.

'Right,' Leslie said, addressing Gwilym, 'this is the procedure. We lower you into the water, just to see if it's got any leaks –'

'Me?' Gwilym looked stricken. The others stared back at him. 'Nobody said anything about me going down in it!'

Pete brought forward a wheel with the ropes and hoses attached. George stared at it. He asked Leslie if he had any idea what parts should be attached to where. Leslie didn't answer. He prised open the crate, revealing the rubberised canvas diving suit, the lead-weighted boots, the metal collar plate and the brass helmet.

'Bloody hell,' Pete whispered.

'Deckchair said Jacques Cousteau wore this,' Leslie said brightly. He turned to Gwilym, giving him a push. 'Get into it, it'll fit you. No need to take off your clothes.'

Gwilym was stiff with resistance. 'I'm not risking going down in that. Not until we know it's waterproof.'

'That's what we're all here for!' Leslie pointed out. 'If you want a share in the salvage, you'll get in the suit. Now.'

Gwilym still hesitated. The others watched him, waiting. To encourage him Leslie picked up the telephone handset and told him he could talk to them through it.

'We'll have that end,' George pointed out. 'He's just got a mouthpiece.'

Leslie nodded as if he had known that all along. He replaced the telephone and glanced out at the sea.

'Hang on . . .' He narrowed his eyes, looking harder. He could see the dim shape of a fishing boat. 'That's bloody Mitch Morgan,' he said grimly. He turned to Gwilym again. 'You're going in that suit right now. No arguments. This is urgent.'

It took them ten minutes to get the suit on Gwilym and another five to fit the boots and manoeuvre the breast plate into position the right way round. Gwilym stood swaying in the outsize suit with his head poking out of the hole at the top, waiting for Pete to bring the helmet. Even in the dark Gwilym looked pathetic.

'It stinks,' he said, trying to angle his nose away from the fumes rising off the suit's interior. 'I'm going to get claustrophobia in here. Can't I just sit on the bottom of the steps with my body in the water and my head above?'

No one was listening to him. Pete brought the helmet and positioned it above Gwilym's head. He lowered it carefully, helped by George, then the three of them set to screwing it in position. They attached the pipes and ropes, pausing regularly to refer to the heavy old instruction manual. When everything appeared to be ready, George picked up the telephone handset and Leslie rapped the glass view hole.

'Can you hear us?' he shouted. He held up a line. 'If you get a leak, tug this. Just tug it once, twice, and we'll haul you back.'

'I should bloody well hope so!' Gwilym's voice squawked from the telephone.

He tried to move to the end of the jetty and discovered the weighted boots were too heavy for him to lift. Leslie, Pete and George staggered with him to the edge, his feet dragging on the boards. They held on to him while he turned and eased one foot on to the iron ladder, then the other. Pete ran back to man the reels and the hand-operated air pump. George stood with the telephone pressed to his ear, marvelling at the fact that he could hear Gwilym's anxious breathing.

'My God, it weighs a ton,' his voice rattled from the earpiece.

'That's so you can walk along the sea bed,' Leslie called to him.

'No, Les, really?' Even over the phone the sarcasm was thick. 'Is that a fact?'

Pete reeled out the pipes and the signal line as Gwilym slowly disappeared below the surface of the water. Leslie began to get excited. He shook George vigorously by the hand and went back to fidget on the edge of the jetty, unable to stand still.

After a minute's slow turning, the wheel suddenly began to whip round. Pete lost control. He watched the stabilising rope come off and go sliding along the jetty.

'Keep your eyes open you two!' he yelled. 'The rope's come off the wheel! Get hold of it!'

Leslie did a rugby tackle but missed the rope by inches. It slithered off the edge and into the water. The three of them stared down into the darkness, seeing nothing.

George jammed the telephone to his ear. 'Are you all right, Gwilym?' He frowned for a moment, then laughed, nodding. Gwilym was still upright and relatively stable. 'He says he just found his old bicycle. Have a listen, Leslie.'

Leslie didn't hear. He was looking out to sea again, watching the faint vanishing shape of Mitch Morgan's boat. He was seized with a sensation of imminent loss, like a man watching burglars break into his house, and being able to do nothing about it. He pictured the greasy Mitch Morgan, imagined his trespassing glee as his rotten old boat chugged nearer the big marker buoys.

'I've a good mind to report him,' he muttered. 'They've got no right to be out there. Look at them, they're going for the wreck . . .'

Gwilym had waded out a few yards in the shallow water, his bubbles making a visible trace. His heavily gloved hand came out of the water, the thumb pointing up.

Leslie saw it and shook himself. 'Great,' he said, bustling around, rubbing his hands. 'All's well. Haul him back in. Let's get out there after them.'

Leslie and George began winding the wheel with the air line attached. Pete snatched up the manual, ran his finger down the page, then stared out at the water. 'You shouldn't have touched that,' he said.

'Eh?'

'You've inflated him. Look.'

Ten yards from the shore, Gwilym floated on the surface like a ghostly Michelin man.

'Shit,' Leslie said.

11

The extra unintentional air pressure had perhaps been a blessing, or so Pete decided as he helped stow the last of the diving gear back into the van. Either it had weakened the suit, or it revealed a weakness that could have been the end of poor old Gwilym if he had gone into really deep water. Whatever the case, the suit had deflated suddenly after they stopped pumping air into it, and now it was leaking badly in three places. The air pump didn't seem to work properly now, either. The mission was a write-off.

Leslie and George shut the back of the van and Pete got in behind the steering wheel. Gwilym stood beside the van, swathed in a blanket and dripping water, his hair plastered flat to his skull. He had been soaked through by the time they hauled him back. He had been badly scared, too, since the only air left to breathe had been in the top six inches of the helmet.

'You want a lift back, Les?' Pete called. 'It'd mean we could get an early start, for a change.'

Leslie looked at his watch. It was a quarter to five, with a hint of light in the sky. He shrugged and stared out over the water.

'Sorry it didn't work, Les,' Gwilym said glumly. 'At least we gave it a good shot. Well, I did.'

He got into the van. Pete asked Les again if he

was coming. Leslie shook his head, still gazing out to sea.

George stepped forward and put his arm around the big man's shoulder. 'Come on, Les, let's go.'

Leslie sighed heavily. 'Do you know why I've been so keen on the salvage, George? So downright *obsessed* with it? It gave me – it gave all of us – an incentive, something for the future.' He shook his head slowly. 'We'd have heard by now. We're not going to get that big boat.'

'We might. You don't know for certain.'

'I've been dreaming about it,' Leslie said. 'Like a fool. Bloody stupid, I suppose. I should have listened to Hughie.'

Pete started up the engine. Leslie and George stayed where they were.

'My Grandad, Old Parry,' Leslie said, 'when I came over to see him when I was a kid, he was always filling my head with stories about wrecks and fortunes. "There's gold out there son," he'd say, and I'd go back to Dublin carrying his dreams. It's funny, I never thought I'd end my days here.' He sighed again. 'Maybe it's just the Irish that dream.'

'We all have them,' George said. 'That wreck will have made a lot of men think they'll make their fortune, but reality isn't anything so easy. The job was out of our league.'

'But it's in that jail-bird Mitch Morgan's league, is it? Do we just stand by and watch him coin it in?' Leslie shook his head. 'I'm not through. I haven't given up yet.'

George turned away, spreading his hands and shrugging at Pete. He climbed into the back of the van. As it pulled away he leaned out. 'Don't go doing anything stupid, Les,' he shouted.

'I'm going home,' Leslie told him. 'All right?'

Out by the marker buoys, with the sky still dark enough to give them cover, Mitch Morgan and Griffith Taylor surfaced by the rowing boat tethered to Mitch's fishing boat. Both men were in full diving gear. Griffith was clutching the end of a rope. He swam the few yards to the side of the fishing boat and as he approached his brother Tom leaned down towards him, brandishing a hook on a pole. Griffith pushed up his mask and took the regulator from his mouth.

'What have you got?'

'Something Mitch wants out of the way,' Griffith said, winding the rope over the end of the hook. 'Tow this out a mile or so, drop the rope and come back for us. Anchor the rowing boat here before you go, in case there's an emergency.'

Griffith watched as Tom tied the rope to the rail and started up the engine. 'Remember,' he yelled, 'come back for us!'

He watched the boat move away, then swam back to the rowing boat where Mitch was bobbing, his arms hooked over the side. 'Are you sure about this?'

'What do you think?' Mitch said. 'If word gets out there's a stiff down there, they'll delay any salvage op for months. But if we drag it out and dump it, it saves everybody a lot of aggravation. You ready?'

Griffith nodded. He pulled down his mask, took a deep breath and put the regulator back in his mouth. They dived in unison, leaving behind dark whorls on the water.

*

As the night wore further towards morning, Geraint Gower was invited to repeat his story about the dead man, in the finest detail he could manage, to a number of other police officers who had turned up at Penrhys Police Station. As his style got under way the tale grew more dramatic and imaginative. He went into graphic particulars of deathly fingers trailing across his back in the gloom of the creaking wreck, and the terror frozen for an eternity in a dead man's staring eyes. While Geraint was talking, Ernie Hardy called the station to tell Barry Mitchell that he had found an old Post Office van with clothes and spare diving equipment stashed inside. On the strength of that, Barry decided it was time to get out on the water and see what was happening.

At that point Geraint abandoned his story and told Barry he was a pompous time-wasting prat who should learn to listen to what he was told in the first place. Barry, embarrassed in front of colleagues, countered by telling Geraint that in the vexing matter of a certain crate addressed to the non-existent Penrhys Aqua Club, he was likely to find himself facing charges of fraud, on top of whatever they threw at him for violating the ban on diving out by the wreck.

At that point David Thomas rushed into the station, hot for a story, his shirt hanging out of his trousers. As soon as Geraint saw him he switched back to his dramatic mode.

'Are you arresting me, Barry Mitchell?' he cried.

Barry blinked at him, startled.

'Well go on then, do it!' Geraint roared. 'Because I'll sue for wrongful arrest! I'll bloody sue, see if I don't! You're calling me a liar, that's what it boils down to!' He turned to David Thomas. 'I told him about the body hours ago.'

As David excitedly checked his camera Barry came striding round the end of the counter.

'Get the hell out of here David Thomas! And you, Geraint, sit where I told you to!'

As Geraint shuffled to the bench and picked up his mug of cold tea, the beginning of pale daylight spread over Penrhys. The place was waking slowly, and out on the water Leslie Parry was steering his little boat towards the marker buoys.

He had been taking it slowly, scanning the water around him for minutes on end until his eyes ached. He had seen nothing. Now, suddenly, he saw two things at once. He cut back the throttle, slowing the boat, and looked again. Mitch Morgan's fishing boat was on the move, a quarter of a mile away, heading west trailing something on a rope behind it. Nearer to hand a rowing boat was bobbing close to one of the marker buoys.

Leslie didn't know what to do. He felt he should follow the fishing boat, but the rowing boat was intriguing too; he revved the engine and moved closer. He was less than ten feet from the rowing boat when a diver broke the surface and pulled up his mask. He swam across to the boat and fumbled over the edged, grabbing a long knife from the debris in the bottom. Leslie recognised him. 'Oi!' he yelled, feeling his temper flare. 'This is Government property, Griffith Taylor!'

Griffith turned towards Leslie's boat and pulled the regulator out of his mouth. He waved frantically. Leslie saw something was wrong. He steered the boat nearer and Griffith came to the side.

'It's Mitch,' he panted, spitting water. 'He's trapped down in the wreck. I can't get him loose, I'm going to cut off his cylinders, that should free him. He's only got a couple of minutes of air left.' Griffith slapped the side of the boat, pointing urgently. 'Rope. Give me the rope.'

'Hang on a minute,' Leslie shouted. 'It'll kill him if he comes up too fast.'

'No, no, it's all right. We were only at twenty feet. Give me the rope. I'll go as slow as I can.'

Leslie turned and snatched up the coil of orange rope. He passed the end to Griffith, then sat down and slipped on his life jacket.

'As soon as you feel a tug, pull him up,' Griffith said.

He dived. Leslie paid out the rope, letting it slide between his hands. Six feet from the end it stopped moving and he gripped it tight. For what seemed a long time he half sat, half lay by the side of the boat, waiting, hanging on to the rope. Then there was a sharp tug, so fierce he almost lost his grip. He began pulling, hand over hand, fighting the drag as wet rope began to coil on the bottom of the boat.

Mitch finally broke the surface with the rope tied under his armpits, Griffith supporting him.

'Help me . . . He's unconscious, I can't lift him . . .'

Leslie tied another rope to the side, giving Griffith something to hang on to, then he dragged Mitch to the side of the boat. Bracing himself, he locked his hands around the unconscious man's chest and hauled him into the boat. Mitch landed on his back, the regulator lolling from his mouth. Leslie pulled it clear and began mouth-to-mouth resuscitation.

'Is he OK?' Griffith yelled. 'Les, is he alive?'

Leslie moved back sharply as Mitch jerked, sat upright, his eyes wild and scared looking. He began to retch.

'Steady now,' Leslie said, bending over him, supporting his shoulders. 'No need to panic.'

'I'm OK, I'm bloody OK, just let me breathe . . .' Mitch coughed once then bent forward, clutching his stomach. 'Oh, God . . .'

Leslie turned as a hooter sounded. It was Tom Taylor coming back in the fishing boat.

'Thank God for that,' Griffith said.

Leslie looked at him, then watched the other boat approach, wondering why Tom had taken it away in the first place.

Getting Mitch on board his own boat seemed to be a priority. Leslie went along with that, although he wanted to ask some questions. The transfer was straightforward, a simple matter of deploying physical strength. Within five minutes Mitch had been pushed bodily up the side of his boat into the waiting hands of Griffith and Tom. Throughout the operation no one had said much, but Leslie had noticed that young Tom looked scared.

As they got Mitch safely on board, Tom grabbed his brother's arm. 'There's Coastguard,' he said, speaking low, 'a police launch, too. The place is going to be swarming. I heard it over the radio . . .'

Mitch, deathly pale, shuddering with cold, slapped Tom on the shoulder. 'Get us the hell out of here,'he ordered. He turned to Griffith. 'We've got to leave. Right now. If there's cops, I'm not getting involved. If it gets out we moved a body we'll be arrested.' He turned and slapped Tom again. 'Get the engine going! Move out!'

Leslie was between the two boats, holding on to the rails. He had tried to patch some sensc together from what they said, but it didn't add up. 'What's going on?' he shouted at them. 'Did you find something down there?'

'It'll blow over,' Griffith told him. 'They won't find nothing. It was weighted down and towed away out over there.'

Leslie looked at Tom.

'I don't know what it was, Les, I just towed it out, that's all . . .'

'Shut it!' Mitch tried to take a swing at Tom's head, but missed. 'Shut it, you hear me?'

He pushed Tom aside and started up the engine. Then he came back to the side. 'Thanks for everything, Les,' he said. 'Now get out of it. I mean it.'

'He just saved your life!' Griffith yelled.

Mitch sneered and slouched back to the engines.

'If anyone's laying claim to the salvage of this wreck', Leslie shouted, 'it's me and the crew of the Penrhys Lifeboat.'

'Be our guest, Les,' Mitch called. 'She's all yours.'

Tom grabbed his brother by the arm. 'What was on the end of that tow rope? You better tell me!'

Griffith gestured vaguely, trying to lighten the moment. 'It was a diver,' he said.

Tom stared at him. 'Jesus Christ!' He went on staring. 'You bloody idiot! I'm not having anything to do with this!' He turned to Leslie. 'Can I come on board?'

Griffith looked at Mitch, then stepped forward. 'Me too, Les?'

He nodded. They clambered on to his boat. Mitch, getting more haggard by the minute, was trying to put on a scathing smirk. It fell away as his engine stalled.

'Get out of here, Les,' Tom urged. 'The police launches are on their way.'

Leslie started up the engine, shaking his head, sick of the fiasco. As the propeller churned the water Tom drew Griffith close. 'When I towed that thing out, Griff, I didn't know what was on the end of the rope, did I?'

'So?'

'Well, when I dropped the line overboard I tied a weight to the end. It was one of Mitch's weights. It had his name on it.'

Griffith smiled and slapped his brother smartly on the back of the head. Leslie swung the boat round, heading for the shore. As they passed Mitch's boat his engine stalled again.

'Don't forget your row boat!' Griffith yelled at him.

Later, when Leslie had tied up his boat at the jetty, Griffith and Tom gave him a lift to the George in their old truck. When they arrived he got out and thanked them for the ride. Before he turned away he winked at them, a declaration that the morning's business was behind them, a matter to be forgotten. Then he disappeared into the car park.

Griffith threw the engine into gear and was about to drive off when he saw David Thomas running towards them. He was panting as he approached the truck.

'Can you give me a lift up to the cove? They've found the body of a diver up there.'

'Have they, now?' Griffith said, stony faced. He opened the door and got down from the truck. He stood facing David. 'First things first.' He clenched his fists at his sides. 'We don't like you taking liberties with our sister. If you want to keep her out all night, then you put a ring on her finger.'

David was baffled. 'What are you talking about?' he said. 'I'm not taking liberties with Meryl.'

Griffith's hand shot out too fast for David to avoid it. He felt a thudding impact on the middle of his face. A second later he realised he was on his knees. Pain suddenly flared between his eyes as blood spattered the pavement.

'My God! You just broke my nose!'

'Griff,' Tom warned from the truck, 'lay off him.'

Griffith stared at David for a moment, taking in his shock and his pain. Then he climbed back into the truck. He closed the door and leaned through the open window. 'You mind how you treat our Meryl in future,' he told David, 'or it'll be your legs broke next time.' He drove off.

David remained kneeling on the pavement, sick and dizzy, holding a handkerchief to his nose. He was still there when Pete and George drew up in the builder's van. Pete looked at him. 'You OK, David?'

The question sounded daft to him as soon as he had asked it. David clearly wasn't OK. George got out of the van as David rose shakily to his feet. 'Griffith Taylor just whacked me one,' he murmured through the handkerchief. 'I didn't do anything to ask for it. He just did it.'

Pete drove on into the car park and George led David into the hotel. As Pete braked the van and got out, he noticed Leslie shovelling sand into the cement mixer, whistling a shade too nonchalantly.

'Everybody's been looking for you, Les,' Pete said. 'This was the last place we thought of.'

'I decided I'd get an early start,' Leslie said, without breaking the rhythm of his shovelling.

Meryl appeared at the back door of the hotel, helping David Thomas to a bench seat. He had an ice pack clutched to his nose.

'Sit down and keep your head back,' Meryl told him. 'I'm sorry about putting you out here, but she'd go frantic if you got blood on her carpet.'

'He said I'd been taking liberties with you,' David moaned. 'I should have told him I should be so lucky, and it wasn't for the want of trying . . .'

Pete had picked up his shovel and was helping Leslie fill the mixer. He glanced quickly at Meryl. She smiled and went back to mothering David.

'They found the body of a diver,' Pete told Leslie. 'Big drama going on – police launches, tugs, and you won't believe this . . .'

Leslie went on shovelling, looking interested but detached, as if the news was entirely an external matter.

'That Mitch Morgan was only anchored out by the wreck with his engine stalled.'

'Is that a fact? Well, well . . .'

George came to the hotel door. 'It's official,' he shouted, 'Trinity House found the owners of the wreck. Their man's inside, says they'll be handing it over to the insurance underwriters.' He put a hand on David's shoulder. 'You should be up at the cove with your camera, you know.'

David moaned something. George looked at his watch and clapped his hands, all businesslike. 'Into the bar with you, Meryl love. Breakfast if you want it, Leslie, and for you, Pete.'

George and Meryl went back inside. A bedraggled

Geraint Gower, still wearing a blanket, shuffled past the car-park gate. He stopped and came back, glaring across at Leslie.

'The wreck owner's been traced, Geraint,' Leslie told him brightly. 'Nobody can put in a claim.'

'I know,' Geraint snapped, coming into the car park. 'Want to gloat do you, Leslie? Another Geraint Gower cock-up. Laughing stock again, am I?'

Leslie planted his shovel in the pile of sand and turned to Geraint.

'No, Ger,' he said, 'you've got more bottle than I gave you credit for. We all fancied putting a claim in for the salvage.' He shrugged. 'You got there first. It would have been yours. Maybe another time.'

With his anger deflected so neatly, Geraint suddenly became emotional. Tears welled in his eyes. 'Time's running out for me, Leslie. Nothing I do works. I just saw it all in a dream, me claiming it, getting rich ... It doesn't happen like that, though, does it?'

In spite of himself, Leslie was touched. He stepped closer to Geraint. 'I was going to ask before,' he said. 'The fact is, I need a man, some decorating and stuff like that. You handy with a brush, at all?'

Traces of the old lunatic fire returned to Geraint's weary eyes. He swallowed back his emotion and grasped Leslie's hand. 'Give us half an hour and I'll be back!' He moved away, hugging the blanket about him. 'Thanks Leslie! You won't regret it!'

He charged off through the car-park gate. Pete stared, watching him go. He looked horrified.

'You're out of your mind, Leslie,' he said. 'Geraint Gower with a paint brush? Didn't you hear about Doris Evans's fence? He painted the concrete gate posts and half her neighbour's brick wall. He was unstoppable.' Pete shrugged. 'But you pay the wages, I suppose . . .'

'That's right, son.' Leslie picked up his shovel again. 'I pay the wages.'

He had a shovelful of sand half-way to the mixer when his bleeper went. So did Pete's. They dropped their shovels.

George appeared at the hotel door, bleeper in hand. 'It's a shout!' he yelled.

'Let's go!'

Leslie ran through the gate with Pete and George behind him. On the road other men were running, heading for the lifeboat station. Geraint Gower, standing at a bus stop, could scarcely believe his luck. As Leslie swept past he fell in behind, his blanket flying. Life is very odd, he thought, panting down the road behind Leslie's broad back. A day can start off looking disastrous, then it turns out like it's your birthday.

12

Mornings were seldom straightforward for Sian Williams. Getting into the day could take an excruciating effort. It could be such a struggle, in fact, that sometimes she didn't make it and just stayed in bed. Other days, the rare ones, she woke up with a feeling of strength, knowing she could do battle with the darkness and show the world a smiling side right from the word go.

Today had been one of those. Now, at mid-morning, sitting in a cab beside the stodgy, middle-aged driver, she was on a roll, feeling good, ready to take on anything so long as the buzz inside her kept going.

'Nowhere to run, baby,' she sang along with the radio, jerking her head rhythmically, letting the breeze from the open window ruffle her short hair. 'Nowhere to hide . . .' She looked at the driver, who had his eyes fixed on the road ahead. 'I love this. Can I turn it up?'

'Yeah,' he grunted. 'Sure.'

She leaned across and turned up the volume then leaned back in the seat, still singing, watching her reflection in the wing mirror. She took off the Ray-Bans and fluttered her eyelashes. *Just like the young Audrey Hepburn* . . . How many times had she been told that?

'Nowhere to *run*, baby . . .'

Penrhys High Street hadn't changed, so far as she

could tell. Same sea-bleached look about the place, same air of compact lives being lived to some purpose. They passed a girl with her arms piled high with bread. She looked at Sian as if she knew her. Maybe she did, but Sian had trouble at such moments, making the connection, establishing a link with her past. Closing her eyes and bringing back the face, she realised the recognition *was* two-way. The girl was . . .

'Come on, come on, come on,' she goaded herself. Some days bullying was the only way to make her memory work. 'Come on!'

A name clicked up in her head. Meryl. Meryl somebody. Taylor. Meryl Taylor. God, yes, they had been mates. She felt better for having made herself remember. That was a plus point, she would add it to her total at the end of the day. If she remembered to make a total, that was.

Some way ahead, in the boathouse at the lifeboat station, Hughie Jones was easing the spare compass back into its brass case, having oiled it and checked that every moving part was as mobile as it should be. Standing close to Hughie, annoyingly close, was Geraint Gower, who had been spouting a stream of second-hand wisdom about gyroscopes and the importance of binnacle-alignment to the accuracy of nautical instruments. Now that the compass was being safely locked away in its casing, he changed the subject.

'Les is taking this darts match with Aberceri very much to heart.'

'Well?' Hughie glared at him. 'Anything wrong with that?'

'He keeps going on about how if we lose, then Aberceri will get the big boat.'

Deckchair appeared, walking slowly, carrying a steaming mug. 'Tea up, Hughie.' He put the mug down beside the open bag of tools on the bench.

'He says it'll be an omen,' Geraint went on. 'A load of old cobblers if you ask me.'

Hughie was getting seriously annoyed. 'You know that for certain do you, Geraint?'

He reached for the mug of tea, snatched it up and roared with pain as a hacksaw blade sticking from the tool bag raked across the back of his hand. He dropped the mug, splashing tea across the bench and the floor. 'Shit!'

'You all right, Hughie?' Deckchair was shocked. The blade had been clearly visible. 'Hughie?'

'Yeah, yeah, I'm fine. It's only a scratch. Get me a towel will you, Deck?'

'You nearly scalded me,' Geraint muttered. 'Daft bugger.'

Hughie looked older suddenly, drawn and weary. He closed his eyes and massaged his eyelids. Deckchair came back with a First Aid box and a damp towel.

'Thanks.'

Having never possessed a flair for diplomacy or timing, Geraint told Hughie he was turning into a right old butter-fingers.

Hughie looked at him. 'Piss off, Ger. I've got work to do.'

The boathouse door swung open with a bump. The three men turned and looked. Sian Williams was standing in the opening, framed in sunlight.

'Hello Uncle Hughie,' she called.

He blinked, scarcely recognising her. 'Well, now . . .' He went forward, dabbing at his hand with the towel.

'It's young Sian.' He smiled, wondering what reason she could have for being here. 'You're a sight for sore eyes.' He realised what he had said, then remembered he would be the only one to see the grim humour in it. 'What brings you to Penrhys?'

'Just an impulse.'

'Oh . . .' Hughie nodded. 'An impulse.'

He broadened his smile and hung on to it, wondering why the sight of the girl made him feel so anxious, on top of all his other anxiety.

Later, when he had seen Geraint off the premises and detailed Deckchair to do a couple of odd jobs, Hughie talked with Sian and discovered, by degrees, that she expected to stay with him while she was in Penrhys. It did not strike him as a good idea, but for the time being he decided to go along with it, for the sole reason that he could not muster the firmness to tell her it was out of the question.

After a welcoming cup of tea for the visitor and a fresh one for himself, Hughie put Deckchair in charge and took Sian over to his flat. The place was small and not especially tidy, a template for a bachelor dwelling, complete down to such details as a backlog of dishes in the sink and an overflowing laundry basket.

'There's not a lot of room, Sian.'

'That's all right,' she said. 'I'm not very big.'

He put her suitcase behind the door. 'Does, ah, does your mother know you're here?'

'She's on holiday.'

The answer, straightforward as it was, made him uncomfortable. 'The thing is, Sian . . .'

His mouth was drying. It had been so much easier to speak to her when she was a kid. This person was not the Sian he had known, this was a woman, an oddly disturbing woman, and he found it hard to take a direct line with her. 'The thing is, since I've split up with your Aunt Bev, I'm sort of used to living alone.'

The abrupt change in her was chilling. Her smile did not simply drop away, it metamorphosed into a scowl. She snatched up her bag and turned to the door.

'That's fine,' she said, her voice hard, metallic. 'I'll find somewhere else, then. Thanks a bunch.'

Hughie was thrown. 'Hang on, look . . .' He put up a hand, detaining her. 'I didn't mean . . . Just hang on a minute, will you?'

Sian stared at him. Hughie struggled to frame an explanation that would be acceptable. He couldn't manage it. 'Just don't start tidying me up,' he said lamely. 'All right?'

She smiled, as if her mood-shift had never happened. 'Thanks,' she said, making it sound warm.

Hughie dug around and found her a spare key. He showed her where things were kept, roughly, and where she would sleep. She took in everything in silence, content to smile and nod. Hughie found that a strain, too.

'I better be getting back,' he said finally. 'Will you be all right here?'

She nodded. He went out, his stomach churning. He hadn't felt so insecure since the break-up with Bev. It was a terrible sensation, one he had thought he would never feel again, like being under threat from something with no name, no shape.

Back at the lifeboat station he got Deckchair to help him wash the outside of the windows. There was nothing like a bit of physical labour, he remarked, for settling the disposition and restoring a sense of proportion. Deckchair happened to believe the same thing about a good stiff drink, but he kept his opinion to himself and got busy with the leathers and a bucket of soapy water.

They were nearly finished when Geraint Gower came drifting back. He kept his distance, shuffling about and whistling softly, waiting for an opportunity to insinuate himself. Eventually and by prior arrangement David Thomas arrived, carrying a large sheet of stout cardboard that flapped in the wind. He propped it against the boathouse, away from the breeze, then followed Hughie's directions for finding a pot of paint and a brush in the boathouse.

Over the next twenty minutes, painstakingly, watched by Geraint, David painted a sign in bold blue capital letters:

BIG BOAT OR BUST

He stood back when he was finished, admiring the effect. He was aware of Geraint looking too. He was frowning. David felt an explanation would help.

'All those 'B's, Ger, well I've done that on purpose, see? It's called alliteration, like it's a sort of play on words. All the top national rags use it. They've worked out that it grabs your attention. Makes you buy the paper.'

Geraint sniffed. 'Only Page Three makes me buy a paper,' he said. 'That and the football results.'

'He's doing it on purpose, David,' Hughie called. 'Ignore him.'

'Poncey banners aren't going to win us the darts

match though, are they?' Geraint insisted. 'Not when I got word Aberceri have put in a ringer. We're stuffed.'

'A ringer?' David looked shocked. 'Who?' he demanded, not waiting for an answer. 'They can't. It's not allowed.' He looked at Hughie. 'Is it? Rules say only the boat crew.'

Hughie asked Geraint if Leslie knew about this.

'It don't matter if he does. They're having Clive Rees in there, whether he likes it or not.'

Rees was well known for his talent with the darts. Some people said he was good enough to go professional.

'How do they figure they can get away with that?' Hughie said.

'Because we've got Tom Taylor as our best player,' Geraint told him. 'He ain't one of us, neither.'

Before Sian got to the door of Meryl Taylor's house it was opened by Tom. His shirt was only half-way on and a piece of toast jutted from his mouth.

'Hi,' Sian said, giving him a careful smile. 'I was looking for Meryl.'

Tom ripped the toast from his teeth, leaving a piece in his mouth.

'She's at work,' he mumbled, chewing furiously, eyeing Sian from the head down.

'Right,' she nodded. 'Where's that, then?'

'I'll show you if you like.' Tom swallowed the lump of toast. 'I'm going there myself.'

Sian waited the swift two minutes it took him to dodge back inside, adjust his shirt, comb his hair and get a jacket. When he came back he had on his confident smile.

On the way to the George Sian fed Tom's curiosity with titbits. She explained who she was in the barest outline, and added that her uncle was Hughie Jones, the mechanic on the lifeboat. Then she moved the topic away from herself by asking Tom if he was one of the crew.

'Nah. You wouldn't get me on the lifeboat.'

'Why not?'

'Bloody maniacs, the lot of them. Anyway, I can't swim.' He squared his shoulders. 'Will you be staying here long, then?'

'I don't know yet. Why?'

'I thought you might like to get to know me better.'

Sian laughed, but she didn't commit herself to a clear answer. The conversation stayed light until they arrived at the George. It was nearly time for Meryl's afternoon break, so Sian sat at a table in the garden, sipping a glass of wine while she waited. When Meryl finally came out she brought a cup of tea with her. They went through a small ritual flurry of greeting, then sat facing each other, smiling broadly.

'I *knew* it was you in the taxi,' Meryl said. 'It's brilliant.'

Sian sipped her wine slowly, nodding, aware of the way the sun played on her soft brown hair. She believed she looked her best in sunlight.

'What are you working in this dump for?' she said. 'I thought you were going to be a model.'

'I was.' Meryl blushed faintly. 'Well, I got a bit of money when I won Miss Penrhys, but I spent that.' She didn't want to give the impression that her capacity to dream had deserted her. It was easy to sound like a no-hoper. 'David Thomas, he's taken lots of photos of me. Says I've got really good bones.'

Sian was gazing around the garden, wrapped in thoughts of her own. She looked at Meryl hard for a moment, as if she had only just arrived. Her smile came back.

'Feels funny being in these parts again,' she said. 'Did you know I was in London for a bit? At the Dorchester.'

'No.' Meryl looked surprised. 'Hughie didn't say anything.'

'I met Bruce Willis.'

'No!' Meryl almost screeched.

'I was this close,' Sian said, leaning in towards Meryl, making her laugh. 'I was Client Liaison Clerk for the eleventh floor. I had to make sure the right flowers and stuff were in his and Demi's room. I saw him every day for nearly two weeks.'

'God, Sian . . .' Meryl was overwhelmed. 'What did you give it up for?'

A shadow of reserve crossed Sian's face. She seemed to withdraw into herself for a moment, then she shrugged softly. 'I met this rich bloke.'

'Oh.'

'He worked for one of those big law firms on Wall Street. He wanted me to go back to New York with him.'

This, added to the Bruce Willis story, was almost too much for Meryl to swallow. Things like this didn't happen to people she knew. And if something like this really did take place, no girl of her acquaintance could conceivably turn down a rich man. Was that what Sian was saying? Meryl realised she must be looking openly sceptical.

'He was married, stupid,' Sian drawled. 'Of course, I said no. Not before I'd had a good time, though.' She stretched delicately. 'Are there any decent clothes shops around here?'

'There's one in town, a bit expensive. We could go to Cardiff on Saturday, if you like.'

'Let's go and have a look now.'

'Sian, I can't,' Meryl laughed. 'I'm free tonight, though.'

Sian stood up, threw her bag over her shoulder and gave Meryl an air kiss, which Meryl found puzzling. 'I'll see you, then.'

'Yeah,' Meryl said. ' 'Bye.' A thought occurred. 'Come with us to the fairground later, will you?'

Sian didn't reply. She wandered off, free as a bird. Meryl watched her, wishing she could do that, too.

It had been an afternoon for callers, Leslie thought. Earlier, he had been polishing his bike when Edward Thorpe drove up in his old Rover and announced, conspiratorially, that he had an insider at HQ in Poole.

'As soon as they made a decision between us and Aberceri, he'll let me know.'

Leslie had asked him if he had any idea which way it would go. No, Thorpe said, but just in case his mole heard anything while he wasn't around, he was investing in a dedicated line. Leslie had no idea what that was.

'For a home fax machine,' Thorpe explained. 'Very reasonable they are, nowadays. He's going to fax me in code. It'll simply say Big Boat, or Inflatable.'

Some code, Leslie had thought. Thorpe added that he thought the scheme also displayed a certain degree of dedicated professionalism. Leslie had asked if it was certain that the RNLI meeting was on the day of the darts match with Aberceri.

'Fourteen hundred hours on the dot,' Thorpe confirmed.

'It's an omen,' Leslie told him.

That had been early in the afternoon. Now Hughie had wandered into the yard while Leslie was loading paving slabs on to the back of a truck. It wasn't entirely unusual for Hughie to do that, especially on a nice sunny day like today, but Leslie got the feeling something was bothering him. If it was, Hughie would come out with it in his own time. Or not, depending on how the mood took him. You couldn't make many predictions where Hughie Jones was concerned.

He watched Leslie working for a few minutes, then he told him his niece had come on a visit, and passed on what Geraint had said about Aberceri putting a ringer into their darts team. Leslie looked amused.

'It's hard to believe Geraint and his big mouth have actually come in useful for once.' He dumped down one stack of slabs and picked up another. 'Well, if that's Aberceri's game, we'll be ready for them. We've still got you and Tom.'

Hughie shifted his feet uncomfortably. 'Don't count on me, Les. I'd hate to let you down.'

'You never have yet.'

'No, well . . .'

'Is your niece staying long, then?'

'Shouldn't think so. Quick visit.'

'I didn't even know you had a sister.'

'I haven't,' Hughie said. 'Sian's Joan's daughter. The ex-wife's family.'

'Blimey.' Leslie dropped a pile of slabs on the truck and raised an eyebrow at Hughie. 'Wouldn't have thought she'd be happy about her staying with you.'

'I don't think she knows,' Hughie sighed. 'I'm going to go over later on, clear it so there's no bad feelings. Last thing I want is Bev at my throat. Any excuse, these days.'

There was a silence. Hughie did not find it easy to talk about close personal matters, not even with Leslie.

'You don't want your niece here, do you?' Leslie said.

'No, no, I don't mind.' Hughie didn't sound convincing. 'She used to be a bit of a handful . . .'

'How?'

'Like kids are. I expect she's grown out of it.'

Leslie felt it was time to cut this short. His pace was slowing and Hughie clearly hadn't managed to say all he wanted to. Neither of them was winning.

'Right.' Leslie clapped his hands sharply and attacked another stack of slabs. 'I'd better get on, then. Vera's in one of her organising moods, she's trying to schedule me to death. I feel like one of those time-and-motion experiments. If Geraint's still at the boathouse, tell him I could do with a hand.'

Hughie nodded. 'I'll do that.'

Neatly dismissed, he waved to Leslie and walked out of the yard.

13

The dazzle of the fairground got brighter as the sun went down, and as the wind dropped the sounds intensified, a clashing of music and machine noises, a garish, strident assault on the nerves. Shouting to make himself heard, David Thomas ordered four hamburgers from Bronwen Pugh. Tom Taylor, Meryl and Sian stood beside him at the van. As Bronwen piled on the onions Sian winked at Meryl and started coaxing Tom again, as she had been doing before he suggested they have hamburgers.

'Come on, Tom,' she said, 'there's not a Welshman in the world who can't sing.'

Not true, Tom insisted: there was just one, and it was him.

'You can sing,' Bronwen said, leaning through the servery gap in the side of the van. 'I've heard you in the George after a few too many.' She handed Meryl her hamburger. 'That's a pretty scarf, love.'

'It is, isn't it? Sian bought it for me today.'

The gift had been made without ceremony, thrust at her like an afterthought, yet the scarf was obviously expensive, it must have cost the kind of money Meryl would never have spent on herself. Not for a scarf, anyway.

'You can sing, Tom,' Sian insisted again as David passed across her hamburger.

Once again, Tom said he couldn't.

'I'll help you,' she offered.

'Help all you like – I can't sing.'

Sian took a huge bite from her burger and chewed heartily. She seemed to be brimming with energy. 'Listen,' she said, 'I've got a good Welsh song.'

'No, please,' Bronwen howled from the van. 'Not Men of Harlech . . .'

'No, no, something much better,' Sian said. She stepped back, spreading her arms dramatically, and began singing: 'I saw the light on the night when I passed by her window . . .'

She hooked her arm through Tom's and forced him to join in. Bronwen watched as all four wandered off into the crowd, singing 'Delilah' at the tops of their voices. She felt a tremor of pleasure, seeing them look so carefree, the way young people used to look before it was compulsory to go around miserable all the time. Sian, it seemed, had descended on Penrhys like a blessing.

So it was odd, Bronwen thought, that the girl gave her such an uneasy feeling. It was nothing definite, nothing she could even describe to herself, except that it was the way she felt just before she came down with a cold, or the 'flu.

Hughie's own uneasiness about Sian hadn't let up all day. That evening, washed and shaved and wearing a clean shirt, he walked over the hill to the neat row of cottages where Bev lived, determined to explain matters to her and make it clear he had nothing to do with Sian coming back, or with her deciding to stay at his place.

As he walked he could hear the sounds of the fairground on the warm air, a far-off jangle, strangely melancholy at that distance. Or maybe it was just him feeling sorry for himself, he thought. Perhaps he was doing the Welsh poetic thing, turning every sight and sound into a poignant commentary on his situation.

Reaching the little house he stood for a moment, clearing his throat, patting his hair. When he pressed the bell the living-room curtain twitched, there was a small commotion inside, then the door flew open and young Debbie came charging out. 'Daddy!'

She leapt off the step into his arms, hugging him. For a moment his heart seemed to fill his throat and he couldn't speak. He held her close, smelling the clean freshness of her hair. *My child . . .*

'Hello, precious,' he said huskily.

'Mummy didn't tell me you were coming.'

She was seven now and bright as they came. Hughie kissed her cheek and held her away from him for a long second, printing this latest image of her on his mind.

'She didn't know, poppet,' he said, 'I just came on the off-chance. I needed to see her about something.'

A fat, sulky-looking teenage girl appeared in the doorway. 'She's not in,' she said. 'She's gone out with Bob. I'm Debbie's baby-sitter.'

'Oh. Well . . .' Hughie shrugged. 'I should have rung first, I suppose. Listen, it's fine, I'll call her tomorrow.'

'I'll tell her,' the girl said. She watched Hughie hover. 'It's Debbie's bedtime.'

'Right.' He put Debbie down and ruffled her hair. 'Night night, then . . .'

Having once suffered the tearing pain of losing his daughter, he was surprised to find that this simple parting was too much for him. He looked at the baby-sitter.

'Can I come in? Just to read her a story? I won't stay long.'

'I can't,' the girl said. 'I'm not allowed.'

Debbie went in and the baby-sitter closed the door. Hughie stayed there for a while, isolated, trying to keep the small pain in proportion.

He walked the couple of miles to the boathouse and got there just as the last ribbons of sunlight were trailing on the horizon. He sat down with his back against the wall, sighing gently, surprised at how loud his own sounds were in the stillness.

This could be paradise, he thought.

Peace, the sea, a sense of purpose, and friends within reach. A man could be measurably happy with very little, so long as he hadn't lost much to begin with. That was a vital element of contentment, he decided; you should strive to possess just a little, and make sure you lose nothing that you value.

Seeing Debbie and knowing he would have to walk away from her again was just one ache piled on a lot of others. One dark morning years ago, out there on the sea, clinging to the rail as the waves crashed across the lifeboat's deck, Hughie had experienced what he believed was called an epiphany; there hadn't been a vision, but he had felt a powerful sense of purpose, a certainty of his own worth that did not need explaining. He wanted to feel that now. He wished – the intensity amounted to longing – that he could feel even a shade more than useless and a failure.

It was turning cold. He climbed up to the coast road and walked slowly back home, trying not to think, finding every thought too bruising to cope with.

Outside his door he paused with the key in his

hand. He could hear voices. He put his ear to the door and heard a man say, 'When's Hughie back?'

Who was that? The voice was familiar, certainly, but in these surroundings it was a puzzle.

'God,' Sian gasped. Hughie pressed his ear harder against the wood. 'You don't waste much time, do you?'

'Let's go into the bedroom . . .'

The man's voice was deep and tremulous, and suddenly it clicked with Hughie. It was Tom Taylor. Tom Taylor was in there with Sian, and there was no sign of a light below the door.

'No,' Sian said. 'Tell me first.'

'I have done.'

'No, you've got to say it properly first.'

'All right, all right.' Tom groaned. 'I love you. OK?'

Hughie put the key in the lock, twisted it and shoved the door open in one swift movement. He flicked on the bright overhead light.

'Say good-night, Tom,' he growled as the couple on the couch sprang apart.

Pete got the story from Tom next morning. He passed it on to Leslie, an hour later, as they worked on the porch extension at Leslie's house. Vera was nearby in her wheelchair, cutting roses for the house and laying them one by one on the gravel path beside her. According to Pete, who spoke softly so Vera wouldn't hear, Hughie had walked into his front room just as Tom was on the point of mounting the recumbent Sian.

'Dirty beggar,' Leslie said, grinning. 'Still, as long as it doesn't affect his throwing. I bet Hughie was none too pleased.'

'She was a right moose at school, that Sian,' Pete said. 'But not any more.'

As Pete went to fetch the wheelbarrow a telephone warbled. Vera snatched up the cordless handset from her lap and extended the aerial. She muttered into the mouthpiece, listened with her face screwed up, then shouted to Leslie that it was for him. He went across, wiping his hands.

'Who is it?'

'Edward Thorpe.'

'This could be it!'

'What? A call-out?'

'No. His mole at Poole HQ. He might have heard already about the big boat.'

'Oh,' Vera grunted. 'Is that all . . .'

Leslie took the phone from her. 'Yes, Edward?'

'It's in, Les,' the bank manager said, his voice hushed. 'Could you send me a fax to make sure it's fully operational?'

Leslie deflated visibly. 'I'd love to Edward, but I don't have a machine.'

Vera screeched suddenly. Leslie turned.

'You stupid, clumsy idiot!' she howled, waving her arms at Pete, who had just run over her roses with the wheelbarrow. 'You clown! Get away from there!'

Pete was scrabbling on the gravel, trying to rescue a couple of blooms from the tangle.

'Just leave them!' Vera howled. '*Leave them*!'

'Look, I'm sorry . . .' Pete stood up, watching the hysterical woman throw herself about in her chair. 'I didn't see them, OK? I'm sorry. Jesus!'

'I'll call you back, Edward,' Leslie said, and switched off the telephone.

'I told her I'm sorry, Les . . .'

'It's all right,' Leslie murmured. 'Clear the wood away from the porch, will you? Just leave this with me.'

As Leslie set about placating his wife, a short distance away another relationship was about to resume after an aborted launch. Tom Taylor, stripped to the waist and sweating freely, was working in the small yard behind his house, transferring a pile of scrap metal to the back of his van. As he hoisted one half of a fractured rear axle he paused, aware someone was watching him. He turned and saw Sian standing at the gate. Lowering the axle again, he wiped the sweat from his forehead with his arm. 'What are you doing?' he said.

'Watching, that's all.' Sian blinked slowly, just once. 'I wanted to see you, but if you'd rather I didn't . . .'

'I didn't say that.'

The line of tension between them was still there, though not as strong as it had been the night before. Sian took a small step forward. 'Want to go for a drive?' she said. 'I've got Hughie's car.'

Tom had a fleeting, intense image of being alone with her again. His stomach shifted. But then his sense of duty buzzed a warning. 'It might be difficult,' he said.

'Why? There's no one else here.'

'I've got to get this stuff over to the yard,' he said, stepping closer to Sian. 'And you're right, there's no one else here.'

He moved in close and put his arms around her. She stiffened. For a moment he tried to kiss her but she wouldn't co-operate. He stepped back. 'I don't know what you're getting so precious about all of a sudden.'

'I'm not getting precious,' she said.

'Looks like it to me.' Tom kicked a stone across the yard. 'I'd better get on.'

He turned to the van again, aware she was still there, still staring at him.

'See you lunchtime, then?' she said in a small voice.

'I'm meant to be at darts practice.' He looked at her and shrugged. 'It's for the big match against Aberceri. Les roped me into it.'

'How convenient.' Sian's face hardened. 'It's a bit sudden, isn't it?'

'No . . .' The quick drop in her mood puzzled Tom. 'I just forgot to tell you, that's all.'

'Please, Tom . . .'

He stared at her, surprised by another transformation. She was smiling, looking unbearably lovely, her arm outstretched behind her, finger pointing to Hughie's little red car.

At one o'clock, the bulk of the Penrhys team who were scheduled to meet Aberceri at darts – Leslie, Hughie, Geraint, Gwilym and George – were gathered in the bar at the George Hotel. Meryl served them their pre-practice drinks as they traded slanders and strove to get the feel of being a team. Leslie, as captain, let it be known that his main man was Tom Taylor, and he was going to put him up against Clive Rees, Aberceri's star.

'That's if Tom bothers to turn up,' Geraint muttered.

David said he hoped Tom would have the strength to lift his darts. The remark gained him a small laugh from the team and a hard look from Meryl.

The practice began badly. Hughie, standing with his

toes squarely on the oche, threw a dart straight into the double five, producing jeers all round. His defence was that he was using the wrong flights. He threw again and missed the board completely.

Things went a little better after that, although there was general annoyance about Tom not showing up for practice. While George was taking his turn, Leslie asked Hughie if Tom might possibly be with his niece.

'God knows,' Hughie said. 'She wasn't talking to me this morning.'

' 'Course he's with her,' George murmured, aiming his third dart. 'Wouldn't you be? I'd be there like a rat up a rope.'

Hughie reassured Leslie that Tom was a good player, practice or no practice; he wouldn't let the team down.

'Famous last words,' Geraint said.

'It's a plain statement of fact,' Hughie told him.

In spite of the liberties taken on his couch the previous evening, Hughie wanted to defend Tom. Instinct told him that anyone Sian fancied would need all the support he could get.

'Let's try and be a team without him,' Leslie suggested. 'Just in case.'

Hughie swallowed the best part of a pint and tried to concentrate on the darts, but he was too unsettled to fix his attention. He was beginning to realise that his life, before his niece showed up, had been really rather placid.

At his next turn he threw no better than before. He went to the bar, ignoring the jeers, and ordered another pint.

Taking his drink to a quiet corner, he sat down and confronted the enigma of Sian. As she was now, a moody and capricious adult woman, she had caused Hughie a few rushes of memory. He recalled Bev's long bouts of moodiness and unexplained crying in the early days of their marriage; there had been his mother-in-law's black moods whenever she had a drink, and there was a general tearfulness in the women of the family whenever emotions came to the fore. He recalled, too, another girl his wife's age, a cousin, who had a tendency to break down in shops and on the street, without warning, and had to take tranquillisers all the time.

Hughie sighed. He had thought that was all behind him, no longer a part of his life. Closing his eyes for a moment, he could still see the way Sian had looked at him last night and this morning, the malice in her eyes, a grudge close to violence. With her, he was sure, there was more than a family tendency to nerves. Sian was seriously disturbed. He knew he wasn't imagining it.

14

If Hughie had known where Sian had taken his car and the darts team's star player, his uneasiness might have flared into panic.

Sian had set off in a bright, animated mood, driving herself and Tom along the upper coast road for several minutes, then out across a picturesque, undulating grassy field on top of the highest cliff on the rocky shoreline north of Penrhys. Twenty yards from the edge she had parked her car on a slope and simply sat there, gazing out through the windscreen at the sea.

Puzzled by what looked like another dip in her mood, Tom had taken the initiative. He reached for her and drew her close, and for a few minutes she was like a doll in his arms, accepting his embraces, letting him kiss her face and neck. When his hand dropped to the hem of her skirt her knees parted slackly. He began kissing her more intensely, but the instant his fingers touched her thigh she recoiled, pulling away to her own side of the car.

He sat back, panting, glaring at her. 'What is it with you?'

'I don't like you being rough, that's all . . .'

Tom groaned. The situation suddenly struck him as ridiculous. Worse than ridiculous: daft. Here he was on a clifftop with an emotional yo-yo who wanted him one minute and rejected him the next, when he could have been back at the George having a decent game of darts and a pint.

'There's such a thing as being committed,' Sian said, without looking at him.

'Eh?'

'If caring is worth anything, it's total.' She looked at him. 'You want to have my body, don't you?'

'Well, I'm not sure I'd put it that bluntly –'

'But you do, don't you?'

'Yeah . . .' Tom nodded, then nodded again. 'Yeah, of course I do.'

'But you don't want *me*, is that it?'

He stared at her big round eyes, wanting to touch her again, cautious in case she pushed him away.

'I think you're losing me again,' he told her.

'I'm saying you want the physical me, the body I live in, but you don't want the me that's in here. The real me.'

'I didn't say that.' *Maybe she's crazy*, he thought.

She was staring at him, not blinking, looking as if a great deal hung on what was being said between them. 'Do you want me, then?' she whispered, frowning. 'Really and truly?'

'Of course I do.' Tom's voice sounded weak to his own ears. 'Definitely,' he added, making it stronger.

Sian smiled. It was like the sun coming out from behind dark clouds. This trip might not be a dead loss after all, Tom thought.

'So you do want me, the total me, you really do . . .'

He nodded.

'To have and to hold, from this day forward . . .'

Tom stared at her.

'That *is* what you mean, right?' she said.

'What?'

'For better for worse, for richer for poorer, in sickness and in health . . .'

'Marriage?' Tom sat forward. 'How could I mean anything like that? I mean we've known each other less than a couple of days . . .'

She was gazing at the sea again, her face grim. 'That's it then, is it?' she said.

'Well . . . What do you want me to say, Sian?'

'I thought you were serious.'

'Whatever I am . . .' Tom felt lost. 'It's a bit soon to talk about getting married. It's stupid.'

He turned, watching her lovely profile as she sat erect behind the wheel, a fine film of tears in her eyes. He reached out his arm to comfort her.

'Get your hands off me!' she screamed.

'All right, all right.' Tom threw himself back against the door. 'Just calm down.'

He folded his arms and turned away from her, staring out at the grass. Sian moved in her seat and there was the sound of a spring relaxing, then the car suddenly began to roll forward.

'Jesus!' Tom clutched the dashboard as the car picked up speed. 'Stop!' he yelled. 'Stop it! What the hell do you think you're doing!'

Sian gripped the wheel, staring straight ahead as the car hurtled to the cliff edge.

'For Jesus' sake! Put the brake on! Sian! *Sian*!'

Tom tried to grab the brake but she clawed his hand away.

'Sian! This is crazy!'

The car bumped forward, getting faster. Sian let

go the wheel and cupped her hands over her mouth, moaning, 'Tom, Tom . . . Just . . .'

'Put the bloody brake on for Christ's sake! Sian!'

He braced his hands on the windscreen as the front wheels rolled over the grassy verge and out into open space.

'Jesus God –'

Sian screamed as the car left the cliff edge and dropped, turning over once before it hit the water. Tom felt the jolt in his spine and a terrible pain sliced through his head. Then there was nothing.

At the darts practice, Hughie had managed to throw another double five. Geraint spoke up amid the general groaning. 'Don't let Hughie throw against Clive Rees. It'd be embarrassing.'

'And I suppose you could hold your own against him,' Hughie retorted.

'I could do better than you.'

'Tell me,' Hughie said, 'is there anything you can't do bigger and better than anyone else?'

'Yeah,' David Thomas piped up, 'get a proper job.'

Geraint turned on him, his face crimson. 'What did you say? *What did you say*?'

He grabbed David and marched him backwards towards the wall.

'It was a joke,' David cried. 'I was joking!'

'All right,' Leslie said, getting between them, 'pack it in, the pair of you. We're meant to be on the same side.'

Geraint had no intention of letting this pass. He tightened his grip on David's collar and threw back his free hand, bunching it into a fist. At that point all their bleepers went off.

'Call-out!' George shouted, grabbing his jacket from behind the bar. 'Call-out! Fight abandoned!' On his way to the door he slapped David on the arm. 'That saved you a trip to the hospital, eh?'

The car was more than half submerged. It had hit the water twenty feet out from shore; the tide was coming in so there had been no direct impact with the bottom. Tom was slumped back in his seat, unconscious. Sian had tried for several minutes to get the door open but it wouldn't budge. She kept on trying, whimpering, frantically tugging at the handle, aware that the level of water inside the car was getting higher. She could also see that the rising tide was carrying them out to sea.

The Penrhys Lifeboat had been at sea ten minutes before they sighted the car being buffeted by the waves.

Leslie used the high-power binoculars to check the registration number as it fleetingly cleared the waves. 'It's your wagon, all right, Hughie.'

The two men looked at each other. Speculation was out of the question. A car was in the water and there might be people inside. That was the fact, the only fact they could entertain at present.

It took another five minutes to get the lifeboat close to the car. By that time only a small air-space remained inside. There was a distinct danger it would sink.

Leslie surveyed the situation from the deck of the lifeboat. 'We should be able to get in there all right,' he said, more for Hughie's benefit than from any belief that it could be done.

In the car Sian still battled with the door, swallowing mouthfuls of water, blood streaking from her broken nails. Every few seconds the water washed completely over Tom, who was still unconscious and deathly pale. Sian made one huge and desperate effort, wrapping both her hands round the door handle and twisting it sharply. Pain shot along her arms but the door did not move.

She let go the handle and sank back. It was time to give in. What had to be had to be, combating the inevitable was pointless. She closed her eyes, weeping softly, feeling the water rise along her neck.

The entire lifeboat crew were sizing up the situation. It was obvious that somebody would have to get into the water and try to open the car.

'Geraint,' Leslie called, 'and you, Gwilym, off you go.'

Geraint looked thunderstruck. 'Are you sure?' he said. 'Isn't there some geriatric cripple you'd prefer to do the job instead of me?'

'Shut up Geraint and get on with it!'

A minute later Geraint and Gwilym, with lines attached, leapt into the water and swam out to the half-submerged car. Geraint saw Sian immediately, her face against the window, eyes closed and swollen with crying. As Gwilym swam alongside they saw both her eyes open. She took a moment to see them. They watched the desperation across her face. She was too weak now to do more than lie there, frightened.

Gwilym and Geraint filled their lungs with air and dived. Between them they took a grip on the door handle and tugged on it fiercely. It wouldn't move. They tried three more times then surfaced, their lungs bursting.

'It's no good,' Geraint shouted to Gwilym. 'We're going to have to move them nearer the shore somehow.'

'How?'

'I don't know.'

Gwilym didn't stop to discuss it further. He filled his lungs and dived again. For nearly a minute he struggled with the door handle, jerking and twisting it. He had to give up again. When he surfaced Geraint was bobbing aimlessly, staring at the others on the lifeboat, who were staring back at him.

Gwilym gulped in air through his wide-open mouth and swam to the rear of the car, which was still a couple of feet above the water.

'What are you doing?' Geraint called.

Gwilym saved his breath. Under the waves he got his foot on to the rear bumper and pulled himself up on the back of the car. He turned and lowered himself slowly until he was squatting on the edge of the roof. Using both heels, he began kicking the back window. It thudded like a drum until his right heel came down extra hard and split the glass with a resounding crash.

The inrush of air altered the car's buoyancy and the back end reared up. Gwilym's weight brought it down again quickly. Water began to rush in through the new opening. Gwilym moved fast. He reached inside and hooked his wrists into Sian's armpits, dragging her out of the seat and half-way through the window. Geraint caught her, pulled her free and swam with her to the lifeboat.

Gwilym eased himself half-way inside the car and took hold of Tom. He was a lot heavier than Sian and being unconscious he was no help at all. Gwilym eased the upper part of his own body behind Tom's shoulders and pushed him to the opposite side of the car. As his legs came free and he began to float, Gwilym caught his collar and dragged him out through the shattered window.

'Well done, mate,' Geraint gasped as they dragged Tom between them to the boat. 'Bloody well done.'

Late that evening, Edward Thorpe telephoned Leslie at home and passed on a progress report on Tom. 'He's alive but there's not a chance of him being fit. He's in some sort of coma.'

'But we were counting on him,' Leslie said, as if his protest might change things. 'Tom was the only one who had a cat-in-hell's chance against Clive Rees.'

He stared at the wallpaper above the telephone, reflecting bitterly on the way fate persistently kicked the feet from under people who deserved better. 'What the devil was he playing at anyway?'

'Who knows? They were probably out for a ride and a bit of hanky panky, I wouldn't doubt. The brakes failed, I suppose, and the rest you know.'

'He had no right to be there. It was a darts practice. He should have been with us.'

'I know, I know,' Thorpe sighed. 'These young ones have no sense of responsibility. What about Hughie?'

'What about him?'

'Well, he's probably our only hope.'

'Our only hope,' Leslie said, 'is that Clive Rees falls down and breaks both his arms before tomorrow night.'

Thorpe said he would call again if there was anything worth reporting. Leslie hung up and went into the kitchen. Vera was standing with her hip propped against the worktop, rummaging through a wall cupboard. Leslie took a bottle of beer from the fridge.

'Have you seen my Valium anywhere?' Vera said.

'No, I haven't.'

Leslie glanced at her warily. That was the first time she had spoken to him since the incident that morning with Pete and the wheelbarrow. Maybe now she would listen to an apology. 'Vera, look, this morning – I'm really sorry about your flowers . . .'

'They're around here somewhere,' she said, sweeping a cluster of bottles along a shelf.

'Vera, I said I was –'

'I heard you.'

Leslie opened the cupboard beside the one Vera was looking in and took out a glass for his beer. As he lifted it he saw the bottle of yellow Valium tablets. He picked them up and turned to tell Vera he had found them. Then an idea struck him. He slipped the bottle into his pocket, poured his beer and wandered through to the sitting-room to watch television. And to think over his idea.

15

Hughie scarcely slept all night and at work next day he was too distracted to communicate. In the early afternoon he hired a taxi to bring Sian back from the hospital. She was very subdued and would not look directly at him. Her face and hands were cut and bruised, but a staff nurse assured Hughie she had no serious injuries.

'There we are then,' he said awkwardly as they got back to the flat. 'Sit down now, love.'

He waited until she was seated on the couch, then he sat beside her, resisting an impulse to take her hand. He asked her what had happened.

She looked at her intertwined fingers for a long moment, then she said, 'It was Tom's idea. He said there was a dirt track. I didn't want to, but . . .'

She shut her eyes tightly.

'Then what happened?' Sian shook her head. 'What?'

'I can't remember.'

'Were you and Tom arguing at the time?'

'I can't remember.' Sian looked at Hughie, her eyes pleading, as if he was causing her pain. 'Look, if I say I can't remember, then I can't remember.'

The awkwardness swelled between them. Hughie stood up, avoiding something he knew he didn't want to face. With this girl, he thought, you sensed more than you ever saw. He asked if he should run a bath for her.

'Yes, please,' she said, friendly again, smiling.

In the bedroom she undressed quickly and put on her dressing-gown. Hearing the water run, she sat motionless on the side of the bed, cupping her hands to her mouth just as she had when the car raced towards the cliff edge. She took a long deep breath and let it out slowly, forcing herself not to let go, not to scream. She jumped as Hughie tapped at the door.

'It's ready, love.'

She went through to the bathroom. The air was thick with steam. She took off the dressing-gown and plunged straight into the water, feeling the heat jolt her out of herself, a momentary release – a foretaste, she sometimes thought, of the distance bestowed by death.

She drew her knees up close to her chest, feeling the weight settle on her mind again, a grey, dispiriting, suffocating veil. She grasped the flannel and pressed it to her mouth, muffling the sobs that suddenly shook her. With tears streaming down her cheeks she reached into the bath tidy and picked up Hughie's razor. She turned it in her fingers, watching the light glint along the fine-honed edge of the blade. So slight a thing, that blade, such an insignificant, wafer-thin fragment of steel, yet it had the power to turn order to disorder, shape to shapelessness, agony to peace . . .

In the living-room Hughie was talking to his ex-wife Bev on the telephone. As he had expected, the call was not proving easy, or even manageable. Bev was a woman who hated the orderly or the humdrum. Everything had to be a crisis with her, a cause for drama. He had wondered once or twice if she was maybe just a frustrated actress.

'Bev, now listen . . .' He raised his voice to interrupt her flow. 'She's fine. She's had an accident but she's fine. OK?'

He frowned at the mouthpiece. 'Look, I did try to tell you she was here, I wanted to tell you face to face, but you were out with Bob. Eh? No, I'm *not* checking up on you. I came over because . . .' He realised he was digging himself in deeper and decided to cut it short. 'Look, when your sister gets home, have her call me, will you?'

Bev wouldn't let it go. She wanted to know why she couldn't lead the life of a free woman when the law had decreed that she was just that, free, a woman at liberty to pursue some kind of life the best way she could. As she saw it, Hughie had implied she was a bad mother who should have a curb put on her leisure-time activities.

'I'm not implying anything, Bev. No, I did not, I never did. You're making this up. I didn't ring up to argue with you, I rang up to talk about Sian. Look, just forget it.'

He slammed down the receiver. It was a mystery to him why he did these things to himself. He had known Bev would be unreasonable, she was never any other way. But still he had done it, he had gone ahead and subjected himself to all that aggression and spite. Was he a masochist, or what?

He was cradling his chin in his hands, wondering what to do for the best, when Sian came into the room, wearing her dressing-gown. There was no sign that she had been crying.

'Uncle Hughie,' she said hesitantly, 'could you lend me some money?'

'What for?'

'I want to go out.'

'Now?'

'Yes.'

Hughie took a quick grip on his temper. 'You can't go out,' he said, standing up. 'You've just been in a nasty accident. You could still be concussed or anything.'

'But –'

'No.' He held up his hand, shutting off her protest. 'I'm sorry. What would your mother think of me? Tomorrow, maybe, you can go out for a while. Now, you get yourself into bed, hear me? I'm late enough for work as it is. I'll call you later.'

He went to get his jacket. Sian's eyes followed him as he left the room. Her jaw was set hard.

Later that afternoon, as Gwilym Davies was locking up the front doors at the Regal, he felt a slight touch on his shoulder. He turned and saw Sian.

'Hi,' she said.

He was momentarily lost for words. Sian pointed at the framed poster beside the door. 'Great film.'

Now Gwilym looked even more surprised. 'What – you've just been in, have you?'

'No.' She smiled at him, her eyes warm and soft. 'I've seen it before.'

'It's usually just OAPs in for the matinee,' Gwilym said offhand. As he got over his surprise at seeing her, he began to look concerned. 'How are you feeling?'

'A lot better, thank you.'

'Shouldn't you be resting or something?'

She stepped closer, still smiling, looking large-eyed

and vulnerable. 'I just had to thank you for saving my life.'

'Well, I didn't actually.'

'Yes you did.'

Sian closed her eyes for a moment and swayed. She put out a hand and steadied herself on his arm. 'Ooh, dear . . .' She shook her hand. 'Would you mind walking me home? I feel a bit faint, all of a sudden.'

'I'll call a taxi,' Gwilym said.

'No, really, I'd prefer to walk.'

'Well, if you're sure.'

They walked off together up the road, Sian taking Gwilym's hand.

Establishing intimacy was easy. All she had to do was walk close to him, occasionally squeezing his fingers with hers, letting him feel he was helping her. She talked in a soft fragile voice, once or twice letting her head brush against his shoulder. The wind off the sea was cool and when Gwilym offered Sian his sweater she thanked him and let him help her pull it over her head. The effect was endearing, giving her a childish, attractively vulnerable look.

'So what happened?' Gwilym finally asked her. 'How come you ended up going over the cliff?'

Sian lowered her eyes.

'Sorry,' he said quickly. 'I didn't mean to . . . You'll have enough with the police questioning you.'

'Tom was . . . he was . . .'

Her voice was so soft Gwilym had to lower his head to hear her. 'Well, you know . . .'

'Trying it on?'

'Yes. He got rough before and I managed to stop

him, but this time . . .' She winced delicately. 'I had to fight him off, and somehow when we were struggling, I don't know, the handbrake must have got knocked and the next thing I knew was, he was screaming at me, and we were going over the cliff.'

'You must have been terrified.'

'All I kept thinking was, what am I going to tell Uncle Hughie about his car.'

Gwilym laughed, though his eyes remained concerned, almost pained.

'I don't feel sorry for Tom,' Sian said.

'I wouldn't.'

'He asked for it . . .'

'The whole family's a bit rough,' Gwilym said. 'Except for Meryl, of course.'

'You like Meryl?'

'Oh, yeah.' Gwilym noticed Sian's fingers had tightened around his. 'She's great fun. You were at school together, weren't you?'

A frown crossed her face, then her smile came back. 'I bet you never saved her life,' she said.

'No, I can't say I have.'

They stopped outside the block where Hughie lived. Sian held tight to Gwilym's hand and turned to face him, keeping the length of her arm in contact with his. 'I'd like to thank you properly.'

Her face was so close now he felt her breath on his chin.

'Look, Sian, you've had a bit of a shock . . .'

'Would you like to come inside?' She was nearly whispering. 'Hughie's at work.'

'I think I'd better go.'

She looked stricken. 'I've offended you,' she said.

'No, no . . .' Gwilym was flustered, blushing. 'It's just that –'

'It's all right. I understand. I understand.'

Gwilym was mystified.

'When the time's right,' Sian said. 'When we know each other better.'

'Yeah . . .'

'Fine.'

They looked at each other. Gwilym could think of nothing to say.

'I'll see you tomorrow, then.' Sian let go his hand. 'At the darts match.'

'Yeah.' Gwilym swallowed. 'Right.'

She left him with a lingering smile and went up to the flat. When she opened the door she saw Hughie sitting at the table, facing her, a bag of groceries beside him. He looked grim.

'Uncle Hughie!' she said brightly.

'I came back early. I thought you might be hungry.'

'I went for a walk.'

'So whose is that sweater?'

'Gwilym's. He gave it to me.'

Hughie passed a hand across his eyes. 'Sian, I don't want you to –'

'I'm perfectly all right now. Don't worry.'

'In future,' he pressed on, 'while you're staying with me, you do as I tell you. Do you understand?'

As she stared at him tears welled up in her eyes. 'I just wanted some fresh air. I didn't do anything wrong. Why are you picking on me?'

She turned and ran off to her room, leaving Hughie wishing he had said nothing.

Late that night, when the flat was quiet and Hughie

was fast asleep, his bedroom door opened soundlessly and Sian crept in. She tiptoed to where his trousers were hung over the back of a chair and picked them up. She inched his wallet from the hip pocket. Opening it, she took out four ten-pound notes, then put the wallet back in the pocket. She replaced the trousers on the chair, glanced at the bed to make sure Hughie was still asleep, then tiptoed out of the room.

Tom Taylor still lay unconscious in a bed in a side ward in the hospital. He had been in a coma for fourteen hours. Every thirty minutes a nurse looked in to make sure his breathing was regular and that none of his other vital signs had altered since the last check.

Earlier in the day Meryl had visited him. She sat by the bed holding his hand while David Thomas tried to make her believe he would be all right: 'They wouldn't say it if they didn't mean it,' he kept telling her.

But they had not really said Tom would be all right. They said there was every chance he would pull out of this without harm, but they couldn't be entirely sure.

'Coma's tricky,' a doctor admitted to Meryl when she pressed him. 'It has no rules that anyone's been able to uncover. It comes, it goes. In some cases, sadly, it stays. Not in your brother's case, of course. I wouldn't expect so, anyway . . .'

She was promised that every four hours, until such time as Tom woke up (if he ever did wake up, though nobody said that), a doctor would perform a neurologic assessment on him, making sure he was in technically sound health and not going into any kind of decline.

Beyond that, nothing very practical could be done. Until Tom's brain decided otherwise, he would remain in the darkness and silence of limbo, alone, with only Meryl's prayers for company.

16

The following day being a Saturday, a number of the volunteers were at the boathouse helping with the weekly spruce-up. Gwilym Davies had rinsed the sea water out of his gear on Thursday afternoon and left it laid out on the boathouse floor. Now he was gathering it up, checking each item to make sure it was thoroughly dry.

Hughie, working on the boat, watched Gwilym for a minute, then called out to him, 'Putting in for a new sweater, are you?'

'No, it just got a bit wet. No harm done.'

'I thought you might be missing one,' Hughie said.

Gwilym caught on. He looked up helplessly. 'She just turned up, Hughie. I didn't ask her.'

'Turned up where?'

'At the cinema. I swear it was nothing.'

At that moment a little woman came into the boathouse carrying a huge bunch of roses.

'I think you've got the wrong place, love,' Leslie told her as she stopped to read the card.

'Gwilym Davies,' she announced.

'Oh.' Leslie beamed at her. 'I beg your pardon.' He pointed. 'The man is right there.'

The woman handed Gwilym the roses and left. He looked bewildered.

'I think somebody's got an admirer,' Leslie muttered.

Gwilym took the card off the flowers and read it. He read it again, then looked across at Hughie. 'I promise I didn't do anything. I walked her home, that's all.'

Leslie took the card and read it aloud. ' "My hero. Love for ever, Sian." How touching.'

Gwilym stared at the roses as if they were infested with something. 'I don't want them,' he said.

' 'Course you do,' Leslie told him.

'No I don't.'

'Then I'll have 'em.' Leslie took the flowers and sniffed them loudly. 'I know someone who'll really appreciate these.'

Gwilym tried giving Hughie a smile. Hughie glared at him.

That night the George was geared for entertainment on an uncommonly lavish scale. The Twilight Zone Disco had been hired and the carpet in the lounge had been removed to reveal a small rectangle of dance floor. There was smoke, flashing lights and loud music. George had specified plenty of Abba and Jim Reeves – 'solid stuff like that with a tune to it' – which put a crimp in the DJ's style but still made enough noise to keep the windows rattling.

George's idea was that the ladies would enjoy themselves at the disco while the darts match took place in the adjoining room. The scheme was not carefully thought out. Since husbands and boyfriends would all, to a man, be next door playing darts or cheering on their team, the women were left with the choice of dancing with each other or with strange males. The potential for friction and disorder was lost on George, who was too preoccupied with the need to win the match to be bothered with niceties of disco protocol.

By eight o'clock the place was getting busy. Among the arrivals was Bronwen Pugh, wearing a rose in her buttonhole. She had scarcely time to get her coat off when a coach drew up outside and the Aberceri contingent began spilling out. Among the first off the coach and into the bar was a man of classic darts-playing proportions. He was Clive Rees, Aberceri's big fat star, whose companions, surrounding him like bodyguards, kept patting him fondly on the arms and shoulders. As they all tried to buy Rees a drink at the same time, Leslie Parry slipped away from the end of the bar and went into the men's lavatory.

He was alone. He took an envelope from his pocket and propped it on the ledge at the back of the washbasin with the open neck facing him. From another pocket he took Vera's bottle of Valium tablets. He tipped one on to his hand, put down the bottle and crushed the tablet to powder between his fingers. He trickled the powder into the envelope. He tipped another tablet from the bottle and did the same again, hunched over as he worked, smiling.

Meanwhile, the two darts teams and their supporters were filling the bar. Meryl and Barbara were serving drinks two-handed. The noise from the disco was so loud they had to lip-read most of the orders.

Pete Pugh managed to sidle alongside David Thomas and ask if there was any word of an improvement in Tom Taylor's condition.

'No, he's just the same.'

'Have they found out what happened, yet?'

'Haven't you heard?' Deckchair cut in. He turned from the bar, carefully balancing a pint in front of him, the froth running over his knuckles. 'I thought it was obvious,' he said. 'They got all carried away, the car started rocking, got into a cycle of perpetual motion and they couldn't stop it. Off it went, off the cliff.'

'There you go, then.' Pete winked at David. 'I always knew he was a goer, that Tom.'

Leslie came out of the toilet and made for the bar. He was intercepted by Vera, who rolled her wheelchair across his path and stopped. She glared up at him and jerked her thumb towards Bronwen, who was standing at the other end of the bar. 'Somebody told me she had some roses delivered this afternoon.'

'That's nice for her,' Leslie said, deadpan.

The tension in Vera was making her shake. But that was nothing new. Leslie believed she was here tonight simply because she derived more from her misery when it was surrounded by other people's pleasure. In her own way, Vera was having as big a time as anyone in the place. Leslie saw Bronwen smile at him and he smiled back. Vera drew in breath like a snake hissing. 'Do you have to rub my nose in it?'

'I didn't ask you to come tonight,' Leslie said.

'Why do you say such hurtful things?' she quavered.

He was taken aback. 'I just –'

'I came here tonight', Vera whined, 'because I know how important this is to you.' She took a shaky breath. 'I shouldn't have bothered.'

Leslie watched her wheel herself away to a group of women near the door. Bronwen smiled at him again but this time he couldn't respond. Vera could do that to him. He turned to the bar and approached the Aberceri darts team, who were clustered at one end.

'John . . .' He reached out and shook the hand of John Davies, the Aberceri coxswain, who was standing with their star player. 'And this is the famous Clive Rees.' Leslie grasped the podgy fingers. 'Pleased to meet you. Let me buy you gentlemen a drink.'

'We've never been known to say no,' Clive grinned.

Leslie caught Meryl's attention and ordered two pints. He smiled at the men as he waited, fingering the envelope in his pocket.

At twenty past eight Edward Thorpe still hadn't left home. He had waited and waited, hoping for a telephone call so he could take word about the new lifeboat – yes or no – to the George. But still the telephone remained silent, the fax machine motionless.

Finally, at nearly eight-thirty, he rang Poole and was told the meeting was still in progress.

'How much longer do you think they'll be? I could hang on five minutes . . .' He listened and sighed. 'All right. In that case, tell them to get me at the George Hotel, or failing that, they can always fax me. Thank you.'

He put down the receiver and took his overcoat from the hall stand. 'I'm going now, Lillian,' he called to his wife. 'I'll be back about eleven. The meeting's gone on longer than expected at Poole, so I've asked them to ring me at the George, but if they can't get me there, they'll fax me. So remember . . .' He opened the front door. 'Don't touch the fax machine!'

He banged the door shut behind him.

Meryl put two pints of bitter in front of Leslie. He paid her, then he told John and Clive to go through and warm up at the dart board. 'I'll bring the beers,' he added.

As the men moved off Leslie moved in close to the bar and took the envelope from his pocket. He tipped roughly half the powdered Valium into one of the pints, hesitated for a moment, then tipped in some more. He looked up and saw Meryl watching him. 'All's fair in love and darts,' he said.

He picked up the glasses and took them through to the darts area. He handed Clive Rees the one with the Valium. 'There you go. Cheers.'

Clive nodded, put the glass to his lips and swallowed nearly half the beer in three gulps.

Leslie smiled. 'Excuse me, fellas, I've got to see to some of my own lads now.' He slapped Rees on the shoulder. 'Finish that up, I'll bring you another one in a minute.'

Rees protested that it was his shout, but Leslie told him not to be silly, he was a special guest, and special guests didn't buy their own beer, not on occasions like this.

By 8.45 the place was packed to the doors. Gwilym Davies had to force his way in and adopt a side-to-side scything action to get across to the bar. Leslie was there, buying more beer. He told Gwilym he was late.

'I had to start the film off. How's it looking?'

'So, so,' Leslie said. 'Hughie's just arrived with his niece. She told me to tell you she's in the disco.' He elbowed Gwilym in the ribs. 'Get stuck in, boy.'

In the disco Sian was making a new local reputation for herself, dancing extravagantly with David Thomas, abandoning herself to the music as David did his sheepish best to keep up with her. As she swayed and writhed sensuously, she eased herself across the floor and began dancing with Pete. Women on the perimeter of the exhibition were trying not to show their displeasure. When Gwilym appeared in the entrance Sian saw him at once and fixed her eyes on him. She kept moving with the music, a faint mesmeric smile on her lips. Gwilym smiled at her nervously, then he turned and went back to the bar. Sian went on dancing, but her smile was gone.

At the bar Leslie was surreptitiously lacing another pint.

'I'll get these,' Hughie said, squeezing in beside him. He took out his wallet and flipped it open, then frowned. 'That's funny . . .'

'Put that away,' Leslie said. 'Tonight is on me.'

Hughie pocketed his wallet and leaned close to the big man. 'Are you sure you want me to play?'

'Why shouldn't I?'

'Well, I haven't been on top form recently.' Hughie paused. 'It's my eyes, Les, they're –'

'You'll be all right tonight. Big occasion, it'll bring out the best in you. Don't worry.'

Hughie was about to protest some more when he saw what Leslie was doing to the drink in front of him.

'Valium,' Leslie confided. 'Clive Rees is going to be so laid back, he's going to have trouble picking up his darts, never mind throwing them.'

In the disco Edward Thorpe whispered something to the DJ and the music stopped.

'All right.' The DJ played a drum roll. 'Ladies and gentlemen, it's that time of the evening. Get ready to rumble! It's the fight of the night, the match of the century! Take your places for Penrhys versus Aberceri!'

People began trooping into the darts area.

'And those of you who still want to strut it out and lay it down dirty,' the DJ went on, 'stay with us here at the Twilight Zone Disco!'

On his way to the darts Gwilym was stopped by Sian. She grabbed his arm and swung him round to face her. 'Are you ignoring me?' she demanded.

'No . . .' He shook his head. 'No, I'm not ignoring you, Sian . . .'

'Come and dance, then.'

'I can't . . .' He wet his lips. 'Not at the moment.'

She propped her hands on her hips and glared at him. 'Why not?'

'Because I'm in the darts team.'

'Let them manage without you!'

She took him by the arm and dragged him through to the disco. Gwilym began to look seriously distressed. 'Sian, really,' he protested, 'I can't.'

She wrapped him in both her arms, holding him close and trying to force him to dance round the floor with her.

'Look, Sian – I have to go.'

She stared at him with big, hurt eyes. 'Is it something I've done?'

'No . . . It's just that . . .' He pulled himself out of her grip and stood back. 'Look. I'll explain later.'

He turned and strode back to the darts match. As he went he felt her eyes in his back, like knives.

17

The first Aberceri player was in position at the oche. Leslie saw Gwilym scurrying through from the disco and pushed him forward. 'Hurry up – you're on.'

Gwilym took a step forward and glanced to one side. He saw Sian sidle up and stand there, watching him.

'Leslie . . .' He felt seriously threatened. 'Listen . . .' There was no way to explain here and now how badly Sian had disturbed him. 'Put someone else on first.'

'What?'

'I need time to settle down. I've only just got here from work.'

'You'll be fine.'

'No. Please.'

Leslie looked at him, saw how unsettled he was. He said OK, he would change the order of play. He went over and talked to Hughie. Gwilym made his way to the bar, aware that Sian was following, still watching him. When Meryl came along the bar he spoke to her like a ventriloquist, his lips barely losing their stiff smile. 'Do me a favour, Meryl. Lean over and give me a kiss.'

She stared at him. 'Why should I want to do that, Gwilym Davies?'

'Because there's someone I'd like to go off me.'

The explanation did not appear to please Meryl.

'So if I kiss you, then people will give you a wide berth.' Her back stiffened. 'Thank you very much.'

'No, she'll just think I'm otherwise attached.'

'Is that so?'

Gwilym looked at her with real pleading.

'Oh . . .OK, then.'

She looked at him for a second, her eyes melting, a perfect simulation of sparked emotion. Grabbing his tie, she pulled him forward and kissed him on the mouth. Sian was watching. So were a number of others.

George Bibby came over and tapped the bar sharply. 'You can pack that in,' he barked. 'This is a bar, not a brothel.'

David Thomas was not pleased either. He stepped up to Gwilym and nudged him. 'What's your game?'

'Sorry, David,' Gwilym said.

'Sorry?'

'I was just trying to –'

'You're trying to get a smack in the mouth, that's what you're doing.'

'He's got woman problems,' Meryl said.

'Has he?' David glared at her. 'Looks like I have as well.'

'It's Sian,' Gwilym said, going ventriloquial again, aware she was still watching. 'She's coming on a bit strong. I wanted to put her off, that's all.'

'Why?' David looked at Sian, then at Gwilym again. 'I wouldn't say no.'

'Oh, great!' Meryl snapped.

Gwilym resented having to explain himself like this. 'I just don't want to know,' he said. 'That's all.'

'I see,' David said, nodding. 'So you start snogging my girlfriend.'

Leslie came to the bar and laid a hand on Gwilym's shoulder. 'Do you feel up to playing yet, or do you want to go for a lie down?'

'No,' Gwilym sighed, 'I'll play. I'm sorry David, I should have asked you first.'

'No you shouldn't,' Meryl said. 'These are my lips, they can go where they like.'

'First game – Aberceri,' Deckchair called.

Leslie pushed his way through the spectators and edged up to Clive Rees, who looked dazed. 'Another drink, Clive?'

'No thanks,' he said thickly. 'I'm fine.'

Leslie turned away, smiling, as the crowd became quiet and Gwilym lined up to throw his first dart. He fixed his eye on the board, his head turned aside a fraction. The dart came back slowly, level with his ear, then he thrust it forward sharply and let it go. It flew in a hard, straight line and landed in number twenty.

At the bar Sian had gone forward and beckoned to Meryl.

Gwilym aimed his second dart. It sailed from his hand as confident and straight as the first one and landed beside it in the twenty.

Meryl noticed Sian and sauntered along the bar towards her.

Gwilym took more time with his third dart. He brought it up by the side of his head and gently moved it back and forward, aligning its tip with the fixed line of his vision. When he was sure his eye and hand were collaborating he threw the dart. It landed, *dub*, in triple-twenty.

The Penrhys supporters roared. At the bar Sian jerked

forward and yelled in Meryl's face. 'You slag!'

The cheering died as her screech tore through the hubbub. 'You two-faced bitch! You're not happy with having one man, you want mine as well!'

She swung a slap at Meryl who stepped back, then leaned forward and swung one of her own. It missed. Sian reached out and grabbed Meryl's long hair, dragging her half-way across the bar. George waded in, trying to separate them.

'Steady on, steady . . . Try to remember you're ladies, for God's sake . . .'

David stepped up to Gwilym and nudged him again. 'Now look what you've done.'

Hughie was standing with a pint glass half-way to his mouth, staring. He could scarcely believe it. The girls were flailing at each other so violently that George couldn't get them apart. Gwilym rushed to the bar and caught hold of Sian, looping his arms round her waist and tugging her backwards. He pulled her away from the bar as George managed to budge Meryl from her stance on the other side.

'Let me go!' Sian screamed.

She wriggled against Gwilym, unbalancing him. He slipped back across a table and sent glasses crashing to the floor. The table tilted and Gwilym fell. He put out his hand and it landed palm-down on a fragment of glass. The edge sliced into the muscle between his thumb and fingers.

'Aah! God!' He howled with pain and rose to his knees, clutching his hand as blood spurted across his shirt.

Sian stood before him, the anger gone from her face. She looked frightened. 'Gwilym? Are you all right?'

'My hand,' he groaned, standing, reaching for a bar towel.

'I'm sorry,' Sian whined. 'I'm so sorry . . .'

Gwilym wrapped the towel round his hand. Sian, watching him, suddenly began to cry. She turned and ran out of the bar.

'What the hell was that all about?' Leslie demanded.

Gwilym didn't feel like explaining. Deckchair called out from the darts area, reminding the crowd that a darts match was still in progress.

'Come on, Gwilym,' Leslie said, 'the game.'

'What?' Gwilym held up his ravaged hand. 'With this?'

'Stupid woman,' Leslie said.

At the bar David watched Meryl finger-brush her hair into place and tuck her blouse back into her skirt. 'Well, that'll teach you,' he said.

'Shut up, David.'

She moved out from behind the bar and went towards the door.

'Where are you going?' David called.

'To find her, of course.' Meryl paused by the door. 'She was in a right state. I want to explain to her. She's my mate. And Gwilym – that's the last time I do you a favour.'

She pushed open the door and walked out.

Shortly after half-past eight Tom Taylor had begun to rally. By nine he was alert, though confused, and was able to be propped up and take a drink from a glass held by a nurse. When he had finished she took his temperature, then asked him how he felt.

'Sore,' he said.

'You will do. But even so, you were very lucky.'

'I know.'

'You can remember what happened, then?'

'Vividly.'

Pain enveloped him as he tried to sit further up in the bed. He lay back, panting. Glancing at the nurse, he thought she looked kind of stern.

'Your girlfriend can't tell us what happened,' she said. 'So we're all waiting for you to tell us.'

Tom stared at her.

Pete Pugh, who had taken over from Gwilym in the Penrhys team, raised a total of twenty-five with his first three darts. Leslie came up behind him as he turned away from the oche. 'You ever thought of getting some glasses, boy?'

Pete told him to shut up. Nearby, David Thomas was quietly berating Hughie, reminding him that his niece had neatly screwed Penrhys's chances by first removing Tom from the team, then Gwilym, the outcome being serious bodily harm in both cases. Leslie interrupted to tell Hughie he was next to play.

'You'll have to find someone else,' Hughie said.

'Eh?' Leslie looked about him, as if he urgently needed witnesses. 'What is this?'

'I've got to go and find Sian,' Hughie said.

Leslie told him Meryl had gone after her, but Hughie insisted he had to find her himself.

'Game to Aberceri,' Deckchair announced.

Leslie felt grim acceptance settle on him like frost as he watched Hughie leave. Turning, he pulled his darts from his pocket and eased his way through the crowd. He took his place ready to throw.

'Leslie,' Deckchair said, 'you need eighty-nine to draw level.'

Leslie nodded, studying the board, calming himself with the familiar pattern of shapes, colours and numbers.

The secret, he heard his grandfather's voice say from long ago, *is to look at what you want to hit, then throw the dart at it. Never mind bloody aiming . . .*

The first dart flew straight into double-top. The second followed faster than the onlookers expected and landed in seventeen. The third seemed to stay poised at Leslie's fingertips for a breathless eternity; then he threw it. Double-sixteen.

The Penrhys crowd went wild.

In the dim light of the lifeboat station the regimented rows of protective clothing looked like silent volunteers, ready for an emergency. Sian stared at the systematic, repetitive order. She stared for a long time. It upset her to see such disciplined tidiness. She felt oppressed by the adherence to rule, the subservience to harmony. It fuelled a snarling anger in her.

Hughie's tool bag lay on the bench. Sian pulled it open and rummaged inside. She took out a hacksaw and ran her finger gently along the blade. It wasn't what she wanted. Rummaging again she found a knife with a straight, sharp edge. Hughie had honed it until it was as sharp as his razor.

She took the knife to the tidy line of clothing and stood, hating the completeness and order for a final few moments. Then she lunged with the knife, slashing into coats and sweaters and waterproofs, dividing fabrics and shredding them, hacking pieces clean out, panting and grunting as she worked her way along the row.

It took nearly ten minutes and when she had finished, when she was done destroying every last garment, she stepped back, perspiration running down her face, and began to cry.

As she stood there in the gloom, hunched forward, her shoulders heaving, the door opened soundlessly and Meryl came in. She could hear Sian, but she couldn't see her.

'Sian? Are you in here? It's me, Meryl . . . I've come to say I'm sorry.'

She moved past the gaunt dark outline of the lifeboat.

'Sian?'

Out of the shadows, suddenly, caught by the light from the shaded bulb, Sian was there. Tears shone on her cheeks, but she wasn't crying now. She drew back her lips, baring her teeth at Meryl, stepping closer.

'Why did you do that?' she said. 'Why? Gwilym liked me . . .'

She brought up her hand, and for the first time Meryl saw the long-bladed knife.

18

Hughie walked briskly along the coast road, still looking for Sian. It was dark and a cold breeze blew in off the sea, chilling him, doing nothing to sustain his hope for a peaceful outcome. A couple of times he tried whistling, but the thin wavering notes sounded the precise opposite of cheerful. He soon lapsed into stolid silence.

As he walked his mind kept going back to a phone call he had taken only minutes before he left home for the darts match. It had been Sian's mother, a gloomy person at the best of times, calling to tell him something he did not want to hear. But he had listened, and now he found it hard to convince himself he would find Sian before something terrible happened.

When he was half-way round the harbour a car came along the road behind him and slowed down. It drew level and the driver wound down the window. It was David Thomas.

'What's going on, Hughie?'

David let the car's speed drop to a crawl as Hughie kept walking. 'I don't know where she's gone,' he said.

'She tried to kill Tom.'

'No . . .' Hughie shook his head. 'I think she tried to kill herself.'

'What's wrong with her? Why is she like this?'

'She has manic-depressive psychosis,' Hughie said.

'What the hell's that?'

'She gets depressed, but like really badly.' Her mother had gone into a lot of detail Hughie did not want to raise with David. 'One minute she's up, the next something can trigger her off, and this –'

'Get in, Hughie. We'll look for her together.'

David stopped and Hughie moved round the front of the car. As he was about to get in he stopped, staring along the road into the distance.

'What is it? Have you seen her?'

'There's a light on in the station,' Hughie said. 'Everyone's at the match . . .'

Meryl was frightened. Sian stood directly in front of her, holding the knife at waist level, the blade pointing straight out. For minutes now she had been talking in circles, rephrasing the same obsessive point over and over. Several times Meryl had tried to interrupt her but Sian had just gone on talking, her voice dry and tremulous.

'I knew you didn't love him. I knew that. But he wants you . . . That's it, isn't it? He wants you more than me.'

Trembling, she looked around her slowly, as if she was surprised to find herself here. She took one hand away from the handle of the knife and drew her fingers across her forehead, kneading the skin as if it hurt.

'You see . . .' She put her hand back on the knife and moved it higher, until it was pointing at Meryl's chest. 'I don't want to carry on. I don't have anything to live for.'

She hadn't said that before. Meryl felt the rhythm of her heart change. She opened her mouth, hearing her tongue click dryly against her palate.

'What about the time you were at the Dorchester?' she said, trying to sound bright and encouraging. 'Bruce Willis, remember? That was worth living for, wasn't it?'

'That never happened,' Sian said. 'I made it up.' She looked down at the knife for a moment, then up again. 'Do you know where I really was? In a hospital.'

'Why were you in hospital?'

'I wasn't feeling well. Then when I met Tom, I thought . . . I thought he cared, but he didn't. So I just wanted to end it. That's why I drove the car off the cliff, it seemed the best way.'

'You drove the car off the cliff?'

Sian began to cry. Meryl moved towards her, her hands held forward in a gesture of help.

'It's all right, Sian. It'll be –'

'Don't come near me!'

Sian pushed her sleeves back and held the edge of the knife over her wrist. Meryl saw a criss-cross of old mutilation scars on the skin.

'Don't come near me!' Sian howled again.

Meryl stepped back against the wall. Sian stayed where she was, the knife poised an inch above her arm. She sobbed convulsively for a few seconds, out of control, almost choking on her misery. Then abruptly she began talking again, going back to the same circular complaint, that Gwilym had seemed to like her at first, but now it was obvious he didn't care for her at all.

'He saved your life,' Meryl managed to put in. 'If he didn't care about you, would he have done that?'

'He didn't know me then.'

'He did. He was just too shy to say anything.'

In the gloom Meryl saw Sian blink at her and frown.

She was beginning to listen, she was weighing up what was being said to her.

'Why don't we go and find Gwilym,' Meryl said. 'Let's go back and watch the end of the darts match, eh?'

'I'd really like Gwilym to like me.'

'He does. So do I.' Meryl edged closer again. 'Give me the knife, Sian. We'll go and see him together.' She put out her hand, watching Sian's grip on the handle relax. 'That's it, give me the knife . . .'

Sian turned her hand, offering the knife by the handle. Meryl reached for it. The station door swung open suddenly and Hughie and David rushed in. David saw the knife in Sian's hand and the startled, wary look on her face.

'Meryl!' he shouted.

Sian howled and pulled back the knife. She thrust out her arm and in one sweeping movement drew the blade across her wrist. Blood spurted from the severed veins. She screamed with the pain and dropped the knife. Meryl grabbed her and cradled her in her arms. She glared at David.

'You stupid idiot!'

Hughie, having expected the worst, remained calm. He went to the telephone and called for an ambulance, then came back, got a blanket and wrapped it around Sian. He applied First Aid to her wound until the ambulance team arrived. They strapped a temporary dressing to her wrist, put her on a stretcher and carried her into the ambulance. As Hughie climbed up behind the stretcher he turned to Meryl.

'Thanks,' he said. 'You didn't have to do that, especially after what happened to Tom and all. . . .'

'Yeah, well . . .' Meryl shrugged. 'She will be all right?'

'She'll live,' Hughie said, 'but I don't know if she'll ever be all right.' An attendant asked Hughie to move inside and he closed the doors.

As the ambulance drove away David turned to Meryl. 'I'm sorry,' he said.

To his relief she smiled at him, and as a completely unexpected bonus, she put her arms round his neck and kissed him.

Edward Thorpe had decided to go home from the match early, rather than stay and watch the slaughter. In the hallway he hung up his coat as methodically as he always did, shaking it first, then putting it on his own peg and making sure the sleeves were unwrinkled and the pocket flaps were out.

He turned to go into the living-room and saw a sheet of paper hanging from the front of the fax. He tore it off and read it.

His wife, Lillian, came out of the living-room. 'Oh,' she said, turning to go back in, 'it's you.'

'When did this come?' Thorpe held up the fax.

'Not long after you left.'

'Why didn't you let me know?'

'You told me not to touch, so I didn't.'

He stared at her, lost for words.

At the George, meanwhile, the Aberceri team captain, John Davis, was taking his place ready to throw.

'All right, John,' Deckchair told him, 'this is the deciding game, and you'll be playing Geraint.'

Behind John Davis, Geraint stood nodding to right and left, acknowledging imaginary applause.

John took aim. He breathed in slowly, let it out slowly, breathed in again, held it, and threw the dart. It went straight into double-top. Amid cries from his supporters John turned and gave Geraint a look that implied he would have a struggle to beat that.

Geraint stepped forward. He spread his feet, stiffened his back and brought up his first dart. His eyes glazed over and his arm shot forward. The dart went into double-top. A roar went up from the Penrhys supporters and Deckchair marked the board, showing that Geraint needed only double-sixteen to win the game.

John Davis's second dart was thrown in a silence as thick as fog. He got treble-nineteen. Now he, too, needed double-sixteen to win the game.

The tension produced a small aberration. Geraint's dart hit the wire edge of its target and jumped out again, sticking into the floor.

Slowly, like a bullfighter in full control of his victim's fate, John Davis stepped up to the oche, took aim, and threw, rising on his toes as the dart left his hand. It flew straight into double-sixteen. In the cheering that ensued, Leslie Parry slapped John's back and tried to smile like a good loser, though in truth he could never understand how anybody in his right mind could be any such thing.

Later, as the Aberceri team celebrated their victory – minus Clive Rees, who was sound asleep in a corner – Deckchair squeezed Leslie's shoulder and told him that even if it felt that way, it wasn't the end of the world.

'It could be,' Leslie grunted.

'Well . . .' Geraint threw a challenging look around the others. 'You can't blame me. I was the most consistent member of the team.'

'Shut up, Geraint,' Pete Pugh said.

'What?'

'You heard me. Shut up. Double-sixteen is the easiest shot on the board, and you blew it.'

Geraint's nostrils flared. 'I'll sort you out in a minute.'

'Pack it in the pair of you,' Leslie told them.

Edward Thorpe came rushing into the bar, much too fast for a man of his build and lack of condition.

'We won!' he cried. 'We won!'

'No we didn't,' George Bibby told him. 'We lost. And you saw it coming.'

'No, no,' Thorpe said, waving the fax, his voice rising. 'The boat! We've got the big boat!'

In that instant Aberceri's celebrations came to an end. They looked at each other. There were signs of open-mouthed shock. Three clear seconds of silence passed. Then the lifeboat-men of Penrhys let out a communal scream of delight.

19

A falcon glided in a slow circle high above the crags to the south of Penrhys, scanning the ground beneath for movement. From a hiding place in the gorse a man called Clive Hicks lay propped on one elbow, tracking the bird's flight through binoculars. Even against the glare of the sky he could tell that the dark, elegant shape was a peregrine, the *falco peregrinus*, a male, a ferocious hunter that could smash a rabbit's skull with one jab of its beak.

Clive watched for a long time, followed the flight patterns of countless birds, impressed by the variety of species in these parts. He stayed in the same spot for more than an hour, changing his position from time to time, lowering the binoculars occasionally to ease the strain on his eyes. When he finally stood up he could scarcely walk. He stamped the ground for a while, getting the circulation back, then strode off the way he had come, down the edge of the crags and into a wood at the bottom.

A stranger seeing Clive would not have taken him for an ornithologist, or even, for that matter, a part-time bird-watcher. He had gaunt, hard-bitten features and over-pale, mobile grey eyes; it was a facial combination that gave him the shifty appearance of an unlicensed bookie or a small-time wheeler-dealer, and his lean, wiry frame backed up the impression.

He trod steadily through the woods and almost walked past his car. It was an old Volkswagen hatchback with an RSPB sticker on the windshield, tucked away under the cover of a rambling hedge at the side of a dirt rack. As he approached there was a burst of loud music from the car. He ran forward, jerked open the passenger door and turned off the radio. In the same movement he grabbed the collar of a scruffy-looking boy of ten, dragged him out of the car and smacked the side of his head.

'I told you to keep it quiet!'

The boy leaned back into the car and peeled a wad of chewing gum off the dashboard. He put it in his mouth and chewed furiously.

'You've been sodding hours!' he complained, in a Brummie accent even stronger than Clive's.

'Mind your mouth.'

Clive took the binoculars from around his neck. He brightened. 'Guess who I saw?'

The boy shrugged.

'Mr Percy Peregrine. And down the cliffs, Kieron, I saw merlins. Such merlins. It's a ruddy gold mine. Where's the sarnies? I'm starving.'

'I've ate them.'

'All of them?' Clive's mouth puckered fretfully. 'That was our supper. Well, now we both go hungry.'

He went to the back of the car and opened the boot.

'I want to go to a hotel,' Kieron said.

'Nope. We're going home tonight.'

Clive stowed the binoculars behind a clutter of cool boxes, coiled ropes and folded nets. Kieron sulked, pulling the chewing gum from his mouth in a long string.

He turned and kicked the nearest wheel of the car. 'I want to go to a hotel,' he said again.

'We'll be back, Kieron,' Clive promised, shutting the boot. 'There's Ollie Owls in this wood, or I'm Digby Dutchman.'

Not far along the coast, roughly a mile to the north, the Penrhys Lifeboat wallowed close to a little sailing dinghy that was being driven by the wind and the tide on to jagged rocks under the sea cliffs. The crewmen of the dinghy, both of them day-trippers, were close to panic. The taller of them shouted at the crew of the lifeboat to catch the line this time for God's sake. It had been thrown once and Hughie, reaching out over the edge, had failed even to touch it.

At the wheel Leslie was nearly as anxious as the men in the dinghy. He edged the lifeboat nearer to them, gauging the swell, fearful of getting too close and crushing the little vessel against the rocks.

'Catch the bloody thing, Hughie,' he muttered.

The rope came flying across again from the dinghy. Hughie didn't appear to see it, he was looking the wrong way. Pete, running from the wheelhouse, threw himself full length and caught the rope down by the scuppers. He jarred his shoulder but managed to hold on to it. Clambering to his feet, he leaned on the side and made the rope fast. He turned to the wheelhouse and gave the thumbs up.

Leslie spun the wheel and eased open the throttle. The lifeboat began to move away from the rocks, pulling the dinghy with it.

'What's the matter with him?' Gwilym asked Leslie, nodding at Hughie out on the deck. 'They nearly went on the rocks.'

Hughie was leaning on the rails watching the little boat bumping along in their wake. He was slack-jawed, openly distressed. Pete was about to say something, then he saw Hughie's face. Geraint was not so observant. He strode up to Hughie and demanded to know if he was blind, or what.

Hughie composed himself with an effort. He turned and stared at Geraint as if he didn't know him.

'Hughie?' Pete came closer. 'Are you –'

'Can you hear that?' Hughie said, tilting his head. 'The starboard engine. I'd better take a look.'

He walked off along the deck, leaving Geraint and Pete staring at each other. For the remainder of the call-out he spoke to no one, and when they got back to the station he kept himself occupied and uncommunicative until everyone had gone home.

Next morning at eleven o'clock Edward Thorpe stood up slowly behind his desk, smiling tentatively as Hughie was shown into the office. The meeting had not been arranged in advance, so Thorpe had no idea why Hughie was there. Experience told him, however, that an unexpected visit from a client – especially when the client came into the office wearing his best suit and a tie – could mean a sudden financial emergency, or even a direct frontal approach for a substantial loan. Either eventuality could lead to a strain in relations, so Thorpe kept his smile tentative as he came round the desk.

'Well, Hughie . . .' He pointed to a chair. 'Do sit down, won't you.'

Hughie walked past the chair slowly and looked out of the window. For a minute he just stood there. When he eventually spoke, his voice sounded weary.

'I've not come to talk about money, Mr Thorpe. It's about the boat.'

The wind left Thorpe's sails. He folded his hands in front of him and gazed down at the shiny toes of his shoes.

'I thought I'd rather see you here, away from the boys, like,' Hughie turned and faced Thorpe. 'You probably heard what happened yesterday, on the call-out?'

'No. What happened yesterday? Do sit down, Hughie.'

Hughie crossed the room but remained standing, his hands gripping the back of the chair. He was having difficulty framing his explanation, and after a moment he appeared to give up the effort.

'My eyes are knackered,' he said. 'Useless. This morning I've been to see Doc Lewis for the results of my test.'

'Good Lord, Hughie, I had no idea . . . What's the verdict?'

'I've got glaucoma. Acute, he said.'

Doc Lewis had tried to present the condition plainly to Hughie, using the facts and a down-to-earth tone to deaden the threat in his explanation: there was increased pressure in the eyes, resulting in pressure on the optic nerve, resulting in diminished vision. Unfortunate, of course, he admitted, but not the worst thing in the world . . .

'It's like, well, it's the end of me as a mechanic,' Hughie said now. 'Probably as a crewman as well.'

For once Thorpe's face betrayed his feelings. He looked deeply sad. 'All right,' he said. 'Take a seat now.'

'The doc said it could be far worse. But how could

it be worse?' Hughie dropped into the chair and stared at the polished top of the desk. 'That boat's been my life. How could it be worse?'

Ten minutes later, as Leslie was paying in cash and cheques at the counter, Hughie came out of Thorpe's office. He went straight to the door without seeing Leslie and walked out on to the street.

The girl stamped the paying-in book and pushed it back to Leslie. He stuffed it in his pocket and hurried out.

On the street he looked both ways and saw Hughie in the distance, walking towards the harbour. He ran to catch up with him. 'Now, then,' he said breathlessly, coming alongside, seeing how despondent and how much older Hughie looked. 'What's the trouble, eh?'

Hughie said he didn't want to talk about it.

'You're just not yourself. Tell me what's up.'

Hughie was reluctant, but Leslie insisted, and as they walked he explained about the trouble he had been having, and how it had finally become so bad that in the end he was forced to consult the doctor. Lewis had suspected it was glaucoma from the start, but he had sent Hughie to the hospital for the tests anyway, and in the end the signs all pointed in the same direction, there was no room for doubt.

'I used to worry I'd end up with arthritis,' Hughie told Leslie. 'Nothing like this ever occurred to me.'

At the harbour they stopped by the wall and leaned there, side by side, with the sea wind blowing gently in their faces.

'When I look ahead of me,' Hughie said, 'it's like I'm looking down a dark tunnel with the walls closing in. My uncle had this, you know. I was an idiot not to face up to it sooner. Frightened, see . . .'

'We're all a bit like that,' Leslie said.

'Well, I'm facing up to it now, and I'm bloody terrified. It's my livelihood gone. Everything.'

Leslie wanted to reassure Hughie, he wanted to lift him out of this ditch of despondency on to higher, hopeful ground. It was the lifeboat-man's instinct, although rescue was hardly a possibility. Comfort was as close as he could come.

'You'd be on half-salary pension for a start,' he said. 'That'd tide you over. And if they're able to save your sight as it is now, you'd still be useful on the crew.'

'On shore,' Hughie said.

'Maybe. Having a mechanic on shore is important. We'll need your advice, your wealth of experience.'

Hughie groaned softly. 'Give it a rest, Les.'

'As long as you don't start moping,' Leslie said, his voice mock stern. 'You're not on a white stick yet. Besides, there's the business of your successor to sort out. With Geraint Gower topping the list of applicants, no doubt.'

'Are you still down on him?' Hughie said. 'Isn't he working out?'

'Well . . .' Leslie sighed and dug his hands deep in his pockets. 'I just banked three hundred quid that should have been five hundred. Except on the last job, Geraint decided to tile a bathroom on his own. Nice tiles, Italian terracotta.'

'Well, that's initiative, isn't it?'

'And imagination. He only laid all the tiles upside down.'

That drew a laugh from Hughie, the first in days. 'He's just the man for your firm then, isn't he?'

Leslie tried to look offended, but he had to laugh too. 'Rude bugger,' he said. 'If you did have a white stick I'd throw it away and let you walk into the harbour.'

The day after Hughie broke his news, Edward Thorpe, as Honorary Secretary, issued an announcement: Hughie Jones would be standing down from his job, and interviews for the vacant post of lifeboat mechanic would be held at the lifeboat station in two weeks' time.

At first, after the blow of learning the truth about his sight, Hughie was relieved to have it all out in the open. He could face the world honestly, with his defect declared. There was no more need to put up a front.

After a week, though, he began to feel a deep, wounding melancholy. In part it was physical, like something blunt and hot lodged in his chest; at the same time it was like a grief, heavy, discolouring his spirit. He knew what it was and why it was there, but he could not distract himself from it, or convince himself it would eventually fade.

But it did. Slowly. Twelve days after Dr Lewis had given him the news, he began to notice he was drawing comfort from doing a few little jobs in the boathouse. A kind of peace was detectable in the simple rituals, a relief and absence of strain, like the moment when a headache passes. The word *surcease* came to him; it was used at his mother's funeral long, long ago by the minister conducting the service, when he spoke of the pain of long illness being lifted from her.

Surcease.

Hughie knew what was happening. Time was simply doing its work. But putting a name to the beginning of the end of his misery was important to him. It was another way of being orderly and hanging on to his standards.

He stayed in the boathouse a little longer that day, cleaning and polishing, cherishing the quiet, with only a radio disc jockey for company. He turned up the volume a fraction.

'. . . A few crumbs of comfort as the nights draw in and the days grow ever briefer,' the friendly voice said. 'Cosy nostalgia to warm those twilight hours, here's Acker Bilk . . .'

It was almost too much for Hughie. As the strains of 'Stranger on the Shore' echoed through the beloved space of the boathouse he sniffed and told himself not to be such a big girl. But in the end he had to let it wash over him, the sentimental glow, the sweet sadness of final times in an old haunt.

As he was locking up half an hour later, he heard a car crunching into the parking space. He went round the corner and waited.

Eventually Edward Thorpe appeared. 'I thought I'd catch you, Hughie,' he said. 'I just wanted to let you know that we're holding the interviews here the day after tomorrow. So if you and Deckchair could get the crew room ready . . .'

Hughie nodded, then as casually as he could, he asked if there had been many applicants for his job.

'A fair few,' Thorpe told him. 'Top calibre, some of them.' He smiled. 'Geraint Gower was the first one in, of course.'

Hughie smiled, too. 'Why not?' he said. 'He knows the boat as well as I do.'

At that moment Geraint and his wife Dilys were bathing the children and putting them to bed. Or Dilys was. Geraint moved from doorway to doorway as the process went on, keeping within conversational distance of Dilys and effectively obstructing her. 'You remember, when we first got this place,' he said, 'how we used to say we'd give it up and move back to the flat, or to anywhere, just a roof over our heads, as long as we still had each other . . .'

Dilys pushed past him carrying one yelling infant while another made huge waves in the bathtub. 'I remember,' she said, giving Geraint a sidelong look. 'Why are you asking? You're not planning on us moving out, are you?'

'It wouldn't be the end of the world,' he said. 'Would it?'

'Well, it would be an almighty pain, love.'

She came out of the bedroom in time to see a sheet of water fly over the side of the bath and cascade across the floor. 'Robert! You little brat! Can't you keep an eye on him, Geraint?'

She pushed past again and hoisted the kicking, squirming Robert from the tub, cocooned him in a towel and knelt to dry him. Geraint, impervious to surrounding events, continued to speculate out loud. 'I mean, if we lost everything, I know I wouldn't go back to the black moods, the drinking, or you and me rowing and shouting . . .'

Dilys paused in her drying and looked at him.

'What is this, Ger? Les Parry hasn't sacked you over them tiles, has he?'

'No way!' He glared at her indignantly. 'That business would have folded without me by now, and he knows it. No, I'm looking at the future, Dil. You know how the song goes, "Exaggerate the positive . . ." '

'*Accentuate* the positive, Pet. And you're going a funny way about it, all this doom and gloom. Here . . .' She pushed young Robert towards him. 'Dry his hair, and tell me what you're on about.'

Geraint patted his son's spiky hair with the corner of the towel while the child pushed a finger up Geraint's nose. 'What I'm talking about is the mechanic's job on the lifeboat.' He eased the boy's hand away gently from his nostril. 'I reckon I'm going to get it. Then I'll be a man with a position, and I can stop skivvying for Leslie Parry, and you can stop ruining your eyes doing that sewing stuff for slave wages. The tide has to turn.'

Dilys sighed and took young Robert from him. 'You don't half talk some nonsense, Geraint Gower. Just don't get your hopes up too high again.' She kissed him. 'Go and check supper isn't burnt.'

20

'Hughie's got to realise he's one of the lucky ones,' Doc Lewis told Leslie. 'Once he's had the laser surgery, we should have his condition under control.'

They were sitting at a table in the bar at the George with their pints in front of them. The evening trade was quiet, which suited Leslie and the doctor, although George Bibby had been complaining.

'Sometimes the patient needs ongoing treatment,' Lewis said, 'but his sight's safe.'

'Then there's no reason why he shouldn't stay on the boat?'

'I don't know about that.'

'Why not?' Leslie said. 'The operation's going to cure him, isn't it?'

He was getting ready to probe the doctor further on the topic, but stopped, seeing Hughie and Edward Thorpe crossing the foyer, heading for the bar. Clive Hicks and his son Kieron were also in the foyer, being checked in by Meryl.

'Right Mr Hicks,' she said, 'that's a double room for three nights.'

He smiled and thanked her. Five minutes before deciding to book in at the George, he had made sure there was a fully operational fire escape at the back. He always did that, wherever he and the boy went.

'Is there a telly?' Kieron asked, pulling out his chewing gum in a string.

'There is, young man,' Meryl said brightly.

'And porno videos?'

Clive slapped the boy casually on the ear.

'I'm afraid not,' Meryl said. She looked at Clive. 'Quite the man of the world, isn't he?'

'It must be his mother. She travels a lot.' Clive tapped the RSPB badge on his anorak. 'We're down for a spot of bird-watching.'

'That's nice. Now, will you want dinner downstairs, or in your room?'

Kieron began to say he wanted it in the room, but his father cut him off. 'We've already eaten, thank you.'

'Very well.' Meryl handed Clive the key. 'Up the stairs, first on the right. Sleep tight.'

She smiled and wrinkled her nose at Kieron. He smiled back and trotted off after his father, leaving a blob of chewing gum stuck under the front of the reception desk.

Leslie and Doc Lewis had been joined at their table in the bar by Hughie, Edward Thorpe and George Bibby. Leslie, on his second pint now, was preparing to be expansive and even outspoken on the matter of Hughie and his future with the lifeboat. 'I'll not mince my words.' Leslie folded his big hands on the table and looked squarely at Doc Lewis. 'Once Hughie's had the operation, why shouldn't he be fit and able to resume his duties like before?'

'The point is, Les,' Lewis said, 'we don't know what the result of the operation will be.'

Hughie immediately looked alarmed. 'What do you mean? You said I would –'

'I mean, of course,' Lewis said quickly, 'we do know the operation will halt the decline. But we don't know what treatment will be necessary afterwards.'

'Well that's cheering, isn't it?' Hughie muttered huffily. 'Remind me not to ask you for a straight answer again, Doc.'

Lewis said nothing, determined to avoid an argument. It was hard offering explanations when so much of the ground was foreign to the people wanting answers. How could he discuss with Hughie the importance of glucose tolerance tests to his eventual way of life? Or the significance of myopia and the pigment dispersion syndrome in the treatment and eventual management of his condition? What were the chances of making him appreciate the balancing of post-operative risks, or the advantage in using drugs such as pilocarpine or metipranolol in conjunction with laser trabeculoplasty? Should he baffle him with medical jargon, or reduce everything to simple language and run the risk of being accused of patronising and misleading him? The best answer, always, was to say as little as possible, then retreat into silence.

'The RNLI will look after Hughie,' Thorpe said, addressing Leslie. 'And we've got some good people applying for his job.'

'What, Geraint Gower?' Leslie raised an eyebrow. 'Forgive me if I don't foam at the mouth with enthusiasm.'

George Bibby laughed.

'Watch yourself, Leslie Parry,' Thorpe said, looking censorious, 'or we'll be advertising for a new coxswain as well.'

'That would be no bad thing,' George said. 'It would

give Les time to finish all those jobs he's started all over Penrhys.'

'What do you mean?' Leslie stared at him. 'What jobs?'

'The Mitchells' bathroom,' Hughie said.

'Mrs Pugh's porch,' Doc Lewis added. 'Mrs Jones's roof.'

'And my bloody car park,' George growled.

Leslie studied his half-empty glass for a minute, then looked around the table. 'You people just don't know,' he said pityingly. 'Good work takes time.'

Upstairs young Kieron was sitting on the bed eating home-made jam sandwiches and watching television. He looked up as Clive, naked and soaking wet, peered round the edge of the bathroom door.

'Where are the towels, Kieron?'

The boy swallowed a mouthful of sandwich, pointing at the bags. 'I thought you said –'

'Not yet, for heaven's sake. And the soap!'

Kieron got up and went to his hold-all. He pulled out a hotel towel from the neat pile inside, and one of the complimentary bars of soap. He took them to his father.

'Right. Now make sure you don't eat all them sandwiches.'

The bathroom door closed. Kieron went back to the bed and sat down. He looked at the sandwich packet. There was one left. His hand hovered over it.

Next day they went out early and walked along the deserted rocky beach. It was a bracing morning, cold and bright. Kieron ran everywhere, delighted to have so much space to himself. He found a large dead bird on a rock and called to his father. Clive hurried across and examined the tattered carcass.

'Is it Arabella Albatross, Dad? Is it?'

'No.' Clive smiled. 'That's just Guy Gull, Kieron. And he's dead.'

'Do you want it then, Dad?'

'They're two a penny, gulls. Nobody would want to put that in a case, would they? The albatross, that's a different matter. She's got wings longer than my arms, Kieron. She flies thousands of miles without rest.'

'Would you catch her?'

'No. That's bad luck for you the rest of your life.' Clive hunkered down beside the boy. 'Now then, what are the valuable birds?'

Kieron frowned, concentrating. 'Eagles, flamingos. . . and . . .'

'Our birds,' Clive said, 'British birds.'

'Eagles and . . . barn owls . . .'

'And kites,' Clive added, 'goshawks, choughs. But not plain gulls, certainly not this old specimen.'

Kieron leaned closer to the bird. 'It stinks,' he said, screwing up his face.

'Well, we don't want a honky old gull in our cold box, do we?'

'Honky old gull,' Kieron repeated, liking the sound of it. 'No way.'

Clive took the boy's hand and they walked off, treading carefully around the pools and over the uneven boulders and rocks.

Around noon, Bronwen Pugh found her hamburger van was becoming the most popular attraction at Penrhys's little fairground. She served up hotdogs and hamburgers to an ever-growing crowd of clamouring children and their mothers, and began to wish she had enlisted some help. There was a limit to how much one person could do, and even if she exceeded her own limit she could see a time approaching, fast, when demand would exhaust supply.

She had just dealt with a particularly awkward mixed order when a man's voice rang out above the noise around the van. 'Twenty-four burgers please, love. No onions on six of them, fourteen medium rare, the rest well done.'

'Hang on!' Bronwen yelled, handing over change. 'Who do you think you –'

She looked up and saw Leslie grinning at her. She made a rude face, glad to see him nevertheless. 'What are you doing here? Why aren't you working?'

'My staff are getting on with the work,' he replied loftily. 'I'm doing some managing. Thought I'd buy you lunch.'

'Lunch?' She pushed back a strand of hair. 'You're joking. Look at this load of gannets. You can get in here and help, that's what you can do.'

'Me?' He feigned shock. 'No way. I'm the pride of the Welsh Lifeboat Service.'

'You're bone idle,' Bronwen told him. 'Now get in here.'

The crowd supported the move. Reluctantly, Leslie slunk through the van door and stepped up beside Bronwen. She put an apron on him and handed him a spatula. 'There you are, pride of the Welsh Lifeboat Service.'

He looked down at himself. 'What will people say, Bron?'

'You should have thought of that before, shouldn't you?'

Behind Leslie the hotplate sizzled and the chips spat hot fat at his bare arms. He leaned down into the opening and stuck his head outside. 'Roll up!' he yelled. 'Roll up! Bronwen Pugh's death burgers! Prime horse steak!'

They worked together steadily, a rare pleasure for both of them, an hour-long collaboration that signified more about their harmony than any number of romantic declarations ever would. When the crowds had thinned and finally died away, Bronwen said they deserved a break. She closed the hatch and switched off the equipment. Together they cleaned down the tops and put up the shutters, then decided a walk through the fair would blow the odours of cooking off them.

Bronwen took Leslie's arm and squeezed it as they walked. 'Now,' she said, 'do you want to tell me what brought you here?'

'I don't know,' he said.

'Not love and affection, then?'

'Not really.'

Bronwen laughed. They wandered between the tents and stalls, nodding to people they knew, not caring about being seen arm in arm, which was only proof of what everybody seemed to know anyway. Bronwen said hello to the barkers as they passed, and to the ladies with canvas cash bags on the tombola stalls and the drab merry-go-rounds. The fairground, she noticed, didn't depress her so much when she was with Leslie.

She squeezed his arm again. 'Come on, out with it. What's eating you?'

He hesitated a moment, then said, 'Hughie Jones.'

They strolled on. Bronwen let Leslie take his own time to tell her.

'He's only a few years older than me. And his whole life's been turned upside down. Just like that – bang. Like a car door slammed on your hand.'

'I'm sorry for Hughie,' Bronwen said, 'but he'll survive. We all survive.'

'That's it, though.' Leslie stopped walking for a moment and looked at Bronwen. 'Isn't there more than surviving?' They started walking again. 'Here we are, our best years past, and you're selling burgers, and I'm . . . well, I'm . . .'

'Helping me sell burgers.'

He sighed. 'What happened to our dreams, Bron?'

He looked at her. She was laughing again. 'What did you expect?' she said, gently punching him on the chest. 'You soft fool.'

'I just don't want to look round at fifty,' he said, 'and have nothing to show for my life. Not even be with the person I should be with.'

Now it was Bronwen who sighed. 'We make our beds and we lie on them. Count yourself lucky you can slip into another one now and then.'

'I know, I know . . .' He patted her hand where it lay in the crook of his arm. 'It's worry, that's all. Poor Hughie got me worrying.'

'You don't know about worry. Every time the boat goes out with you and Pete on it, that's worry.' Bronwen shivered. 'If I could have you both serving burgers on land, I would, believe me.'

Leslie stopped and faced her. He tried to give her a hug but she pushed him away. Public displays of affection were all very well, but there was a limit.

'Get off and do some work,' she told him. 'I've got to open up again.'

Back at the George, Clive Hicks sat sipping a half pint of bitter in the bar, studying an array of tourist brochures and maps spread out before him. He spoke to Meryl as she came round gathering up the menus. 'Seals and dolphins,' he said, 'that's what the lad loves. Wildlife and such.'

Kieron was engaged in something surreptitious at the other side of the room.

'You'd find seals in the coves up a way from Penrhys,' Meryl said. 'You'd need a boatman to take you, mind.'

Clive put a nail-bitten finger on the map, pointing. 'What's this little island round the headland? Pen . . . Pendragon, is it?'

'*Pen y Ddraig*. There's all manner of sea birds there.'

'Ooh ah?'

'Guillemots,' Meryl said, 'razorbills, choughs, puffins too.'

'Well . . .' Clive rubbed his hands. 'A little trip round the island might be just the thing. The only islands we have in Brum are traffic ones.'

Meryl explained that her brother Griffith did the lobster pots, and could probably get Clive the hire of a boat for a reasonable price.

Clive beamed. 'Wouldn't that be champion, eh, Kieron?'

Startled, the boy dropped the ashtray he had been trying to slip into his pocket. Meryl glared at him for a second, then she turned to Clive again and smiled. 'I'll take you down to the harbour when

I've finished here,' she said, always keen to help a stranger, and to put a bit of business her brother's way.

21

The little boat was moored by the harbour wall on the low-tide sands, its battered outboard folded in over the stern. Clive and Kieron stood alongside as Griffith Taylor delivered a brief run-through of its virtues: watertight, no ultra-modern, high-performance engine to go wrong, and the hull was the classic shape and size that had served the casual sailor for more than a hundred years. To a trained eye the need for an overhaul would have been apparent, but Clive, snug in his landlubber's ignorance, seemed enthusiastic about the vessel. He tapped Kieron on the shoulder and pointed to the crude lettering hand-painted on the prow. 'Nice name for a boat, isn't it?' He winked furtively. 'Nest.'

Meryl corrected his pronunciation, putting stress on the 'e' and making it longer. 'Nest. She was a Welsh princess.'

'A bit of a nympho, according to legend,' Griffith added.

Clive put his hands over Kieron's ears, a clumsy rebuke that was entirely lost on Griffith.

'She ended up disappearing in Ireland,' Meryl said.

'We won't go that far,' Clive promised. 'Just a little trip round the bay.'

Griffith broached the matter of payment for the hire of the boat.

'Yes,' Clive said, 'I was just going to . . .' He rubbed his hands together, his eyes darting between Griffith and Meryl. 'I'm a bit short of cheques, at the moment, so I thought if this could be put on the hotel bill – part of the service, like?'

Griffith didn't look very keen, but Meryl nodded. 'I think we can do that, Mr Hicks.'

'Champion.' Clive nodded at the boat. 'Tomorrow, then.'

Later that day Geraint Gower presented himself at the boathouse. He made no bones about the fact that he had come to pick Hughie's brains. If he was going to get the job of mechanic, he said, he wanted to supplement his natural talent for understanding machinery with as much solid, old-hand wisdom as he could pick up.

For an hour he dogged Hughie's steps, following as he went about his work, quizzing him on every aspect of lifeboat maintenance and management. When Hughie had answered all the questions, and Geraint could think of nothing else to ask, he sat down on the catwalk and watched Hughie cleaning the slipway rollers. A blissful silence reigned for a couple of minutes.

'Hughie . . .' Geraint scratched his beard thoughtfully. 'If there's any other topic they're likely to ask about, I'd really appreciate . . .' He let his voice tail off.

Hughie stared up patiently at the underside of the boat. 'No problem,' he said.

'I know you'd put in a good word for me, if they were to ask you . . .'

'I don't think they would ask me. They follow their own procedure.'

'Most of the lads would like one of their own to get the job,' Geraint said, introducing a sanctimonious note. 'A Penrhys appointment.'

He was interrupted by a knocking at the door, then a man's voice calling from above, asking if anybody was home. Geraint got up and hurried to the front.

A middle-aged man in a suit was waiting outside the open door. He stepped in as soon as he saw Geraint. 'Good afternoon,' he said, 'I'm looking for –'

'If it's a tour you want, I can spare a few minutes.'

'No, I don't –'

'It's no problem,' Geraint assured him. 'It's our policy to encourage members of the public to . . .'

He stopped talking as Edward Thorpe arrived and shook hands with the visitor. They seemed to know each other very well. Hughie appeared, oil rag in hand. The visitor beamed at him. 'Good afternoon, Hugh.'

'Afternoon, Bob.'

'I'll be down in a jiff,' the visitor said. He pointed up at the crew room. 'Just going over a few things with Mr Thorpe in the penthouse suite.'

When Thorpe had led the way to the crew room and the door was shut behind them, Geraint turned to Hughie. 'Who is that bloke?'

'That, Geraint, is Bob McGaskill.' The name meant nothing to Geraint. He looked blank. 'He's down for the board tomorrow. He's the District Engineer.'

Geraint still looked blank, but he groaned softly.

That evening Edward Thorpe and Bob McGaskill had a drink together in the bar at the George. Geraint had made a point of bringing Dilys out for a drink, too, and as he paid George he looked along the bar and offered to buy the District Engineer a drink. McGaskill thanked him but declined. Geraint waited for his change, pocketed it, then looked along the bar again, beaming sociably. 'You sure now, Mr McGaskill? One for the road?'

'He can hardly have one for the road', George muttered, 'if he's staying the night.'

McGaskill thanked Geraint again and told him he was fine.

'What about you, Mr Thorpe?' Geraint said.

Thorpe shook his head, smiling thinly.

'Don't press the gentlemen too hard,' George said, leaning close, 'or you'll be disqualified for canvassing before you even get near the interview, eh?'

Geraint glared at him, picked up his drinks and took them back to the table where Dilys was waiting.

'Persistent bugger, isn't he?' George said.

'Oh, he's all right,' said Thorpe, keen to make sure none of the candidates for Hughie's job got off to a bad start. 'A rough diamond. Loyal to a fault.'

Across the room, Geraint spent a strenuous minute trying to lip-read what Thorpe was saying to McGaskill. Finally he gave up and tapped his wife's arm. 'Know who that is at the bar with Mr Thorpe? It's Mr McGaskill. Bob McGaskill.'

'Who's he, then?'

'Dilys . . .' Geraint gave her a pitying look. 'He's only the District Engineer. He's interviewing me tomorrow. We already met down at the boathouse, when I was helping old Hughie Jones, poor devil.' He took a long gulp from his pint and wiped his mouth with the back of his hand. 'We got along really well.'

Dilys sipped her orange juice, saying nothing, feeling

Geraint's tension, which intensified as Leslie Parry came into the bar with Pete Pugh. Leslie was greeted warmly by Edward Thorpe, who proceeded to introduce him to McGaskill. The two men appeared to take to each other at once. McGaskill bought Leslie and Pete a drink.

Laughing at something McGaskill said, Leslie turned from the bar and noticed the Gowers. He raised his glass to them. Dilys smiled back. Geraint stared at his beer.

Upstairs, young Kieron Hicks was lying on his bed, watching his father through half-closed eyes. Clive sat on the other bed, methodically rubbing the barrel and breech of his .22 rifle with an oil-soaked cloth. When he had finished he put the cloth in a hold-all on the bed beside him, and took out a telescopic sight. He slid the unit on to the rifle, checking the perspex was clean.

'Dad,' Kieron said, 'I think . . .'

'What?'

'I think you should let the pretty ones live.' He waited for a reaction. 'Dad?'

Clive fiddled with the sight, taking it off and putting it on again. He glanced at Kieron.

'We've got to live too, son. You remember that.'

Kieron did not argue.

Clive took the telescopic sight off the rifle. He looked at Kieron again. 'Besides,' he said, 'this way, lots of people who'd never see the birds, get to see them. In museums and galleries and such like. And it's the pretty ones they want, isn't it?'

Kieron nodded, his eyes closing. He opened them again after a minute and lay watching his father track the rifle round the room, pausing to take imaginary shots at imaginary, valuable birds.

Much later, as Dilys Gower sat up in bed leafing through a magazine, she glanced down at Geraint lying beside her. He was wide awake, staring at the ceiling. 'What's the matter, Ger?'

'Nothing. I'm fine.'

'Is it about tomorrow?'

He went on staring upwards for a while, then he turned to her. 'You know, he skived off work today at lunchtime. Left me and that useless Pete Pugh sweating our guts out.'

Dilys tried to stall his fretting, knowing it would turn into a paranoid sermon on the evils destined to oppose him in his latest quest.

But Geraint had to talk, now that she had disturbed his silence. 'He's the one person that stands between me and that job, Dil.'

'Don't start on about Leslie Parry again, love. You know he won't be on the panel.'

'His influence'll be there, all right,' Geraint said darkly. 'You saw him sucking up to McGaskill tonight.'

'I saw him being introduced to McGaskill. He didn't try and force a drink down his throat like someone else I could mention not a million miles from here.'

'That was just politeness.'

Dilys put down her magazine. 'Look,' she said, 'Leslie Parry has not got it in for you. He gives you work when he can. He pays you.'

'Aye . . .' Geraint nodded vigorously. 'To keep me under his thumb.'

Dilys rolled up the magazine and hit Geraint on the head with it.

'Hey! What's that for?'

'It's for being pig stupid,' she told him. 'Leslie's seen how much effort you've been making, and he's accepted you're part of the team now.'

Geraint considered that.

'You've got to start seeing the good side of him, Ger. Got to start liking him.'

He narrowed his eyes. 'Why?'

'Well, I mean, for years to come you're going to be his right-hand man on that boat . . .'

It was a joke, heavily tinged with expectation. They both laughed.

Next morning Hughie walked to the lifeboat station with the wistful air of a man doing something for the last time. As he opened up the boathouse he heard the familiar sound of Leslie Parry's motorbike. He waited by the door while Leslie parked and came down the steps.

'Come to wish me well on my last day, eh?'

'What do you mean, last day?'

Leslie followed Hughie inside. He watched him stop by the lifeboat and run his gaze along her lines. 'By tonight,' Hughie said, 'she'll have another engineer.'

'Don't be soft,' Leslie told him. 'It's not going to happen overnight.'

'I want it to.' Hughie slapped the hull and faced Leslie. 'A clean break. I'm not hanging around like Deckchair Jones.'

'Don't be too hasty, that's all I'm saying. And if the maroons go up today, you're on the boat with us.'

Hughie smiled and patted the side of the boat. 'I hope he'll look after her like I have, whoever he is.'

'I hope so too,' Leslie said. 'It's just not going to be the same, Hughie.'

Hughie cocked his head, smiling. 'You're the one's going soft, Les Parry. With me gone, that leaves you the next oldest on the boat, and you don't like that, do you?'

'I hadn't given it much thought.'

Hughie made his way up to the crew room, laughing. Leslie followed him.

'You're a bad liar, Les.'

'Maybe I am. Maybe I *have* got used to having an old crock around.'

The crew room had been tidied and cleaned. Leslie stared at the chairs lined up neatly by the table. 'I wonder who it'll be,' he said.

'Geraint's a capable enough mechanic . . .'

'For an amateur. He's got no qualifications.'

'Neither did I, when I started.' Hughie ran his finger along the edge of the table and examined the tip for dust. 'I picked the job up as I went along.'

'Yes, yes, but *Geraint*, Hughie. He's like a stone in your shoe. Always there, niggling.'

Hughie shrugged. 'The point is, he loves the boat. That's what counts.'

Leslie decided to make no more of it. He changed the subject. 'Do you know what you're going to do, yet? After?'

'Nope.' Hughie shook his head firmly. 'I've been living my life like tomorrow's never going to happen. But the next tomorrow is, isn't it?'

Up in the town, well ahead of time, Geraint Gower stood in front of the mirror in his hallway, beard and moustache neatly trimmed, hair combed. He wore his suit, his best shirt and a tie. Dilys picked threads off his shoulders and gave his tie a final twitch. At the door she kissed him for luck. 'Remember,' she said, 'if you get it, I'm proud of you. If you don't, I'm still proud of you.'

Geraint gave her his winner's smile. 'This is where the tide turns,' he said.

22

A smart Ford Escort pulled up in the car park at the George. A woman in her late twenties got out, locked the car and went inside.

Meryl, cleaning in the foyer, looked up and saw the smart-looking visitor stride up to the desk and put down her overnight bag. George, his antennae on full alert, appeared by the desk wearing his hotelier's smile. 'Good morning,' he said. 'Are you joining us, young lady?'

'I'm a bit early,' she said. 'I booked last week.'

'Then you're a bit late, aren't you?'

She waited for George's mirth to subside. Her face stayed expressionless, registering neither amusement nor offence. 'I booked a room for tonight. My name's Sydnie Hully.'

George leafed through the register and found the reservation. 'Yes, indeed. Miss Hully, is it? Ms Hully? Mrs?'

'If the room's free, I'd like to go straight up.'

'Of course.' George looked chastened. 'Of course.'

Meryl watched, amused, as he scurried to get the key.

Further down the town, in the forecourt of a guest house facing the Penrhys seafront, Leslie and Pete were squaring and levelling soil ready to put down patio slabs.

They looked up as a horn sounded. It was Bronwen in her hamburger van, drawing up at the roadside.

'Don't let him slack off, Pete,' she called to her son.

'Me?' Leslie put on an offended face, his hand spread over his heart. 'I'm the only one that does any work around here.'

Pete laughed sarcastically as he manoeuvred a big slab into position. 'He's getting on, Mam. I have to make allowances.'

Pete's grin faded as he saw Leslie's wife Vera, in her wheelchair, being pushed along the pavement towards them by her sister Phyllis. Leslie saw her, too, and looked at Bronwen. She gave him a wry, resigned look as she put the engine in gear and drove away. Leslie turned to face Vera with much the same look. Her chair drew level with them and she raised her hand. Phyllis stopped. Vera then sat back and surveyed the flattened earth in front of the guest house, eyeing it fretfully, as if she could see something wrong. 'I thought this was to be finished last week, Leslie.'

'Sure,' he nodded. 'But we got a bit behind.'

Vera sighed, a theatrical sound of long-suffering, mingled with despair. 'You know you've got to get back to Mrs Evans's porch?'

'Yes, Vera.'

'If you didn't spend all day chatting to . . .'

She tailed off as she saw Pete glaring at her. Phyllis winked at Leslie. 'Come on, Vera,' she said. 'We can't keep Leslie chatting all day.'

Vera snorted and sat back as Phyllis wheeled her away. In silence Leslie turned and slowly flexed his arms. In one movement he snatched up a concrete slab and dropped it on the ground with a satisfying thud, like a muffled gunshot. Pete watched him, feeling a rare flash of sympathy.

Back at the hotel Sydnie Hully had been shown to her room and George had come back downstairs to find Griffith Taylor talking to his sister in the foyer. Meryl saw the question in George's look and explained about the arrangement she had made with Mrs Hicks over the hire of the boat. 'He asked if he could put it on the hotel bill,' she said. 'I said yes.'

George nodded, tight-lipped. 'And I'm expected to pass on cash to your no-good brother here?'

'Well?' Griffith blinked at him. 'I don't see what the harm is.'

'The harm', George said, 'is first treating me like a clearing bank, and second letting my guests go out to sea in something I wouldn't take a bleeding bath in.'

Griffith looked offended. 'There's nothing wrong with that boat.'

'No? Sooner be out there in a sieve, I would. And you, Meryl, don't go making arrangements for the guests without checking with me or Barbara first . . .'

George stopped as Sydnie Hully came down the stairs. She put her key on the desk and nodded politely to the three of them. 'Good morning,' she said, and walked out.

George and Griffith watched her calves until they were through the door and gone.

'That's a cool one,' George said. 'Property speculator. I'd put money on it.'

'Don't you worry about the boat, Mr Bibby,' Griffith said, getting back to the subject. 'Everything's hunky-dory.'

'Hunky-dory.' George made a face. 'I just wish Mr Hicks had settled his bill in advance, that's all.'

Geraint Gower stood in front of Hughie, waiting for his approval. In truth, Hughie thought he looked desperately uncomfortable and ungainly in a suit.

'You look very smart, Geraint. And good luck to you in there.'

Edward Thorpe had come out of the crew room. He looked at his watch, then down at Geraint. 'You're a bit early,' he said. 'But you might as well come in.'

Geraint braced himself and went up the stairs. He let Thorpe close the door behind them and stood watching the top of McGaskill's head as he wrote something on a sheet of paper on the table. Beside McGaskill was the District Inspector. Geraint tried not to look at him at all.

McGaskill looked up and smiled briefly. Geraint tried to do the same, but wasn't sure he had succeeded. He was so nervous his face had gone numb.

'This is Geraint Gower,' Thorpe said.

The two men at the table nodded. Thorpe went round and took his seat beside them. Geraint swallowed.

This is it, he thought, *this is it. Make or break . . .*

Outside two more applicants had arrived. Hughie showed them to chairs set up on the catwalk. The men looked cautiously at each other, and at the single vacant chair between them. They had been seated five minutes when Sydnie Hully appeared. Hughie went forward as soon as he saw her.

'Can I help?' he said.

'I'm looking for Mr Thorpe.'

'I'm afraid he's very busy,' Hughie said, wondering

if this was one of Thorpe's business contacts. 'For the rest of the day, probably. Your best bet is to go to the bank –'

'He's expecting me, actually.'

'But he's doing interviews.'

'Good,' Sydnie said. She smiled at Hughie, walked to where the two applicants were sitting, and sat in the chair between them. Hughie looked bewildered.

Upstairs, after several minutes of routine questioning, Geraint was looking less nervous and was even beginning to feel confident. He had been careful, when giving his answers, to look at all three men in turn. He felt it was a tactic that would give him the edge, along with his obvious natural ability and positive outlook.

'If you found that any additions or alterations were needed to the existing electrical circuits,' McGaskill said, 'how would you proceed?'

'No problem there,' Geraint said, beaming at all three. 'I'm a dab hand with electrics.'

McGaskill nodded. 'Would you need to check with anybody before making the changes?'

Geraint realised he had been on the verge of a bad mistake. 'I mean,' he said, hoping he didn't sound flustered, 'I would check with the District Engineer first, of course.'

To his relief, he saw McGaskill smile approvingly.

More questions followed, then quite suddenly Geraint found himself on the far side of the ordeal. The interview was over. In a slight daze he let Thorpe show him out.

'Thank you, Geraint.' Thorpe pushed past him and called out to where the other applicants waited: 'Sydnie Hully, please.'

Geraint stopped dead as the young woman got

up and walked past him towards the crew room. He watched until she was out of sight, then looked across at Hughie, scarcely able to hold in his laugh.

The atmosphere in the crew room had undergone a measurable shift. Thorpe was as bewildered as Hughie had been, and the District Inspector was speechless. McGaskill, on the other hand, had known in advance that this interviewee was a woman, and he knew about her impressive record of service on another lifeboat. He only hoped she would not expect special consideration because of her sex.

The interview was tough. McGaskill asked every awkward question he could, and whenever Sydnie made a point he would confront her with its opposite, and demand to know how she would respond in alternative circumstances. Sydnie took the interview in her stride, remaining calm and professional throughout. Towards the end McGaskill was the one who looked worn down.

'What would you do if an engine appeared to be losing power?' he snapped, forgetting he had asked the question right at the beginning.

'I'd check the fuel system,' Sydnie said, phrasing her answer differently this time. 'I would see if either the fuel or the air filters were choked. I would check there wasn't a rope around the propeller. If it was –'

'What if it was air in the system?'

'I was just going to say, sir. I'd get it out using the hand-priming pump, and by loosening the bleed screws.'

McGaskill could not find fault with that. He grunted something and stared at his notes.

Thorpe cleared his throat and addressed Sydnie more gently. 'How long have you been an Assistant Mechanic?'

'Three years, sir.'

McGaskill suddenly thought of something. 'How did you get along as a crew member?' he demanded.

'Fine, sir.'

'No problems at all?'

'None,' Sydnie assured him, 'once the others stopped making allowances for the fact I'm a woman. I was part of the team.'

The men at the table looked at each other, wondering what they could possibly ask her next.

The *Nest* had been out on the water since eight-thirty, and now Kieron was beginning to grow tired of the endless monotony of the sea. Clive sat at the tiller, blank-faced, his gun case at his feet. They could be anywhere, Kieron thought, there was nothing in any direction but the waves, the same old grey and blue waves. A change of colour would have been something.

He decided he had been sitting for too long. He moved back from the prow, stepping cautiously as the little boat rose and dipped, testing his balance as he stood in the middle. He discovered that by leaning his weight first on one foot, then the other, he was able to make the boat wallow steeply from side to side.

'Kieron! Cut that out!'

The boy sat down. He stared glumly to right and left and yawned. There was nothing but water. He had never imagined there could be so much of the stuff. 'This is boring.' He turned and looked at his father. 'When are we getting there?'

Clive pointed to the front. Kieron looked. Ahead of them a craggy, barren island seemed to have loomed suddenly out of the sea. 'Five minutes,' Clive said.

As they drew nearer the rocks Clive cut the engine and began, awkwardly, to manoeuvre them closer to the shore using the oars. Kieron stood ready with the mooring rope, his boredom gone, the adventurous promise of the dark, brooding island impelling him forward.

'Right Kieron!' Clive shouted. 'Now!'

Kieron hesitated, looking down at the deep, dark water lapping the boat. He was frightened, but he knew that was no reason to turn back from doing something. He closed his eyes and jumped.

His feet slipped on the seaweed covering the rock and he fell to his knees. But he was ashore. Moving quickly, he wound the rope around a boulder and tied a clumsy knot. Clive clambered out over the prow, clutching a bag, with the gun case on a strap over his shoulder.

'Dad? Where are –'

Clive put his finger to his lips and pointed upwards. Lining the ridges on the steep rocky slopes above them were rank upon rank of gulls, silent since the boat came, nervously aware of the intruders.

Clive and Kieron followed a natural path between the rocks, rising steadily, imperceptibly. After a few minutes Kieron looked behind and saw the boat directly beneath them, looking like a toy.

They kept climbing until Clive found a niche where he could crouch with good arm support, opposite a rockface thick with sea birds. Kieron moved back and leaned on the rock, watching. Clive squatted, took the rifle from its case and fitted the telescopic sight. He repositioned himself and propped his elbow on the rock. With his eye to the sight he scanned the ledge directly opposite, then one higher, then one higher than that. He paused with the gun pointing sharply upwards, the sight centred on two small blue-black birds with red beaks and legs. The rifle steadied as Clive shifted his arms, pulling the stock closer to his shoulder. Kieron held his breath.

The gun went off with a sharp crack. A moment later the air was filled with flurrying gulls, flapping and circling, squawking angrily. On the ledge, one of the small black birds lay motionless.

Clive turned to Kieron and winked. 'Do you know what we just got, son?'

'Charlie Chough!'

'Charlie Chough. What a start, eh?'

The birds continued to wheel in the air above them, screaming harshly. As Clive stood up Kieron leaned forward and was caught by a gust of wind. Looking down he saw the boat bobbing vigorously on its rope. The sea was getting stormy.

'Wait there, son.'

Clive put the rifle on the case at Kieron's feet and stepped out gingerly across the ledge of rock. As he reached the steep incline he repositioned the bag on his shoulder, spread himself against the rockface and started to climb. Kieron watched anxiously as a number of herring gulls began to swoop near Clive. 'Dad,' he called nervously. 'Dad!'

Clive reached the ledge where the dead chough lay. He knelt and looked down at Kieron. 'Don't shout, son. I'll be back down in a second.'

Clive reached out, picked up the limp body of the bird and eased it into his bag.

'Watch out, Dad!'

Clive turned in time to see two herring gulls dive to attack him. He brought up his arms, shielding his head, flinching as the hard, sharp beaks struck at his wrists and elbows. Three or four more gulls joined the pair attacking him, swooping from opposite sides, necks outstretched to peck as they swept past.

Kieron was terrified. Watching his father cower from the gulls he stepped forward impulsively and his foot hit the case. He looked down and saw the rifle. He picked it up. It was heavy for him and his arms were too short to hold it properly, but he aimed it as carefully as he could, pointing the barrel at the rock above the swirling birds. Setting his teeth he pulled the trigger. The gun fired and the slight recoil bumped Kieron's collarbone. He saw the gulls scatter and heard his father cry out as the bullet hit him in the neck.

Clive straightened, clutching at the wound. He tottered as his foot slipped on the side of the ledge. He tried to lean inwards but the other foot slipped and he plunged down the sloping cliff face.

He landed on the flat rocks at the bottom with a bump and a terrible crunching of bone. There was no further sound or movement. He lay there, sprawled and still. Kieron dropped the rifle.

23

For a long time after he climbed down the rock to the shore, the boy was only able to stand there, transfixed on the horrible fact that he had shot his father. He stared at the body, half certain in his terror that he could make time go back, just a little, just enough for the bullet not to leave the gun. He felt himself on the verge of knowing how to do that.

'Dad,' he whimpered.

As he wiped blurring tears from his eyes he saw Clive move. It was no more than a twitch of the arm, making the elbow rise and fall. But it was a sign. It was life.

Kieron ran forward. Clive's eyes were shut. The only hint of life now was a tiny tremor at one corner of his mouth. There was blood on his face and on his hands from the fall, and a thin, terrible line of blood from the bullet wound in his neck. Gulls had landed nearby and were watching.

'I'll get you back, Dad . . .'

Kieron ran across the slippery rocks and untied the boat. He put the rope over his shoulder and tried to pull it round nearer to where Clive lay. His feet slithered on seaweed and bird droppings, but he made progress, easing the boat forward, gaining inches as he groaned against the weight of it.

The boat caught suddenly on a submerged rock. Kieron jerked the rope. The boat jumped forward and Kieron's feet flew from under him. He landed on his backside, the pain of it jolting along his spine and neck. For a moment he couldn't see for the tears blinding him. He knuckled them away and realised he was not holding the mooring rope any longer. He looked up and saw the boat being carried away on the swelling waves, the rope trailing uselessly behind.

He got up and ran after it, but even so close to the shore the water was dangerously deep. He found himself immersed up to his waist, being buffeted from side to side. Water splashed into his mouth and as he struggled to breathe he saw the boat much further out now, wallowing and bobbing as the rough sea carried it away from the island.

Coughing and spitting out the salt water Kieron thrashed himself forward with his arms and found a rocky outcrop. He took hold of it with both hands and pulled himself up, rolling over and sitting on the slimy promontory. Looking over his shoulder he saw Clive still lying at the foot of the cliff, the gulls stalking jerkily around him. 'Dad!' Kieron called, keeping open the helpless line between them. 'Da-ad!' He stood up and ran across the rocks, sliding, falling and getting up again, clapping his hands to disperse the gulls. As he drew near he saw Clive's head move. After a moment his eyes opened. He blinked, then he winced. Kieron's heart swelled in his chest and felt like it might burst.

Leslie came into the kitchen, stained with dust and sweat. Vera was in her wheelchair at the table, a book open in front of her. She did not look up.

'We got that job done, then,' Leslie said. 'I'm just going to have a quick wash, OK?'

Vera said nothing. That was not unusual. Leslie moved past her, heading for the stairs. 'Leslie . . .'

He stopped and waited. She liked a touch of drama in the timing of her statements, and occasionally he indulged her.

'I'm willing to do something for you. If you do something for me.'

'Oh aye?' He stepped close to the table. Vera wrinkled her nose. 'Sorry, madam,' he said. 'Shall I go and bathe first?'

'No. Stay.' She glanced up at him. 'I've been looking at your books.'

'What? Who gave you –'

'Phyllis did. Now shut up. They're a mess, as far as I can see. You get the work, but you don't organise, or delegate, or charge, or account properly. So you're always running round like a headless chicken.'

'Well . . .' He nodded at her solemnly. 'Thanks for that, Vera.'

'I'm prepared to do the books for you,' she said. 'I'll manage the business for you, so you can get out of it nearer what you deserve.'

In spite of himself, Leslie was touched by the offer. 'Right.' He smiled cautiously. 'And what is it I do for you?'

'You stop seeing that woman.'

He stared at her, catching the fierce wounded pride as she stared back. He did not have to consider the proposition. He shook his head. 'I'm sorry, Vera.'

Her hands clenched slowly as he turned and walked out of the kitchen. She stared at the table, catching the corner of her lip between her teeth, biting down until it hurt.

Upstairs Leslie ran a bath, undressed and immersed himself. He lay low in the water, his model lifeboat floating near his chest. The heat eased its way into his muscles and he tried not to think, because some matters were not improved by thought. He knew, without having to resort to any kind of rationalising or arguing with himself, that what Vera asked was entirely beyond him. His relationship with Bronwen caused his wife pain but he could only regret that, he could do nothing to break a tie that was a vital feature of his existence. Vera might as well have asked him to part with a limb.

His bleeper sounded from the pocket of his trousers. He shot up in the water. *Duty*, he thought, hauling himself out of the water, feeling the depression lift. *Thank God for duty*! There was nothing like a real emergency to knock everything back into perspective.

Over at the hotel, in the bar, Geraint switched off his bleeper and downed the remainder of his pint. He looked expectantly at George Bibby.

'Not this one,' George said. 'My legs are playing me up something awful. Will you apologise to Les for me?'

Geraint nodded curtly and headed for the door. 'You might be missing my first shout as Chief Mechanic,' he said, tapping a table as he passed. 'Touch wood.'

At the lifeboat station Edward Thorpe was talking on the telephone in the crew room. Bob McGaskill and the District Inspector were packing up their papers. The interviews were over.

Hughie stepped cautiously into the room. 'Is it all right for me to . . .

'Come in, Hugh,' McGaskill said. 'We're done. Where's Gower?'

'He'll be here shortly.'

Thorpe put down the telephone and McGaskill turned to him. 'If Gower's crewing, shouldn't somebody tell him?'

Thorpe said he would do that. He winked at Hughie. 'You've got a successor,' he said.

Leslie and Pete arrived at the same time. Leslie asked if anybody knew what the alert was about. Nobody responded and he was about to ask again when he saw Sydnie Hully hovering by the door to the crew room.

The door opened and Hughie and Thorpe came out. 'Right Les,' Thorpe called, 'there's a small boat drifting off Pendragon Island. Seems to be empty.'

Geraint came running through the door, showing more energy than usual. He stopped short when he saw Sydnie Hully.

'Gwilym, Geraint, Pete,' Leslie called, 'get your gear on. And you, Hughie.'

They turned to the changing room. Thorpe announced pointedly that they were still short of a muster. 'Miss Hully is in Penrhys for the day,' he added. 'She's also an experienced crew member with another boat. Leslie?'

Leslie hesitated no longer than a heartbeat. He shrugged. 'If it's OK with the boys.'

'Not half,' Pete said.

Gwilym and Hughie nodded. Geraint made no response.

'All right,' Leslie said briskly. 'Now get a move on lads. And lasses.'

While the others changed Sydnie checked along the row of available waterproof clothing. She picked out a jacket and trousers and stood with them for a moment, unsure what to do next.

Gwilym tapped her gently on the shoulder. 'Here,' he said, and handed her a folded pair of jeans and a sweatshirt. 'These are spare. You're more or less my size.'

She thanked him with a smile. There was a swift round of ribald cheers from the others, who were nearly finished putting on their waterproofs and boots. It was obvious they were delaying the final stages of buttoning up before they got on the boat.

'I'm not doing a striptease, you know,' Sydnie said.

All eyes switched quickly towards the wall.

Minutes later, as the lifeboat went down the slipway, details of the emergency were circulating in the town. In the bar at the George, Doc Lewis was confronting Griffith Taylor and Meryl with the facts. He wanted details. George stood by the bar, a smug witness.

'It was a private transaction,' Griffith said defensively.

'It's not very private any more,' the doctor pointed out. 'The boat's been found drifting, empty, about two miles out to sea.'

'Sooner go out in a sieve, I said,' George muttered.

Griffith rounded on him. 'Why don't you belt up, George Bibby?'

'All right, Griff,' Meryl said, appealing for calm. 'It was a man and boy staying here,' she told Doc Lewis. 'Name of Hicks. I think they were heading for Pendragon Island.'

The light was beginning to fade. The rising tide almost covered the rocks around the island, successive waves washing over Clive where he lay. Kieron crouched beside him, trying to be brave, not knowing what to do, using his shirt to wipe the seaweed slime from his father's face and head. The only blessing he had encountered, so far, was that the bullet had penetrated just a short way under the skin of Clive's neck. It was visible at the centre of the oozing wound.

'Kieron . . .' It was the first time Clive had spoken since his eyes opened. Kieron leaned close, listening to the faint croaking of his father's voice. 'My legs are broken. Where's the boat, son?'

'It's gone, Dad.'

Clive reached over his head and gripped the edge of a rock. He strained to pull himself up, but the effort only increased the pain in his shattered legs. He lay panting, waiting for his strength to gather so he could speak again. 'I've . . .' He coughed, making pain flare along his legs. 'I've got to get above this water, Kieron. You'll have to try and move me.'

The boy stepped behind his father and gripped his shoulders. He heaved and pulled, but his father's weight was too much, he couldn't shift him. Their eyes met for a moment, Clive's brimming with pain. Kieron looked down. The water was up to his father's waist. Above them gulls circled, squawking, cackling.

A mile away, in the forecabin of the Penrhys Lifeboat, Hughie was reminiscing with Sydnie Hully. She listened intently as he told her about his early days in the lifeboat service.

'When I started my father nearly disowned me,' he said. 'He ran this garage outside of St Margaret's, and the nearest he ever got to the sea was down at the beach. But for me, the first sight of –' He stopped talking suddenly, listening.

Sydnie was listening, too. 'One of your engines is playing up,' she said.

He tut-tutted. 'It's the starboard again.'

He was already on his way to the engine room. Sydnie followed him.

At the bow rail Pete was scanning the island through binoculars. On the third sweep from east to west he saw a crowd of circling gulls. He focused on them, then lowered the glasses carefully.

'I can see them!' he yelled. 'In the old landing cove!'

Leslie was in the wheelhouse, steering. He acknowledged Pete's report, then looked round, startled, as the rhythm of the engine noise began to break up. 'Hughie!' he shouted. 'One of the engines is cutting out! Hughie!'

Geraint stuck his head round the wheelhouse door. 'We'll sort it out as quick as we can,' he snapped.

'Hang on, Geraint. Who's –'

Geraint had gone. Slowing the boat almost to a halt, Leslie peered out towards the darkening island. No detail could be distinguished. He switched on the searchlight.

Over on the island Kieron had given up trying to move his father. The waves were buffeting Clive now, swelling over the rocks and along his body. Half-demented with his own helplessness, Kieron turned towards the sea and saw the searchlight come on. He leapt to his feet and began jumping up and down, waving his arms, shouting, 'Here! We're here! Over here!'

He kept on jumping and waving, wondering why the boat didn't come any closer.

In the engine room Geraint was literally pushing Hughie aside to get a look at the faulty engine. 'Let me at it, Hughie man. I can sort this.'

Hughie backed off. Geraint eased in and stared at the oil-glistening intricacy of the components. He went on staring, saying nothing. Sydnie hung back beside Hughie, watching. When Geraint had been looking at the engine for nearly a minute, Hughie finally shouted at him above the noise, 'Get back out!'

Geraint jumped up and glared at him.

'Go on! I'm still mechanic on this boat!'

Hughie pushed his way back to the installation and dipped his hands down into the warm innards of the engine. He felt for a moment, then looked up. 'Miss Hully?'

A serious opinion was clearly being called for. 'Fuel pump?' she said.

Hughie nodded. 'I could do with a hand,' he said. 'If you're willing . . .'

Sydnie joined him without another word and plunged her hands in beside his. Geraint folded his arms and watched them bleakly from the doorway.

Up on deck Pete was still monitoring the island through the binoculars. He could see that Clive was being moved around by the water now. The boy was clinging to his father but they both appeared to be weak. Every few seconds the lad looked round forlornly and stared at the light from the lifeboat.

In the wheelhouse Leslie stood by, waiting. Pete and Gwilym were ready to do their bit, too, as soon as they had power.

And suddenly it came. Both engines throbbed back to life. Leslie opened the throttle right up. Gaining full power, he headed for the island.

Within ten minutes they were close, easing towards the rocky shoreline. From the deck Clive could be seen clearly, buffeting about in the water between the rocks, the boy fighting to keep a hold as his father grabbed wildly at the boulders, trying to steady himself.

'He's going under,' Gwilym told Leslie. 'Can you get in closer?'

'Not here. The rocks are like razors.'

As the boat nosed closer a wave threw Clive against a rock. He roared with pain and disappeared under the water. Kieron screamed, a high, pure note of terror.

Gwilym had a lifebelt ready. He checked his line then gave Pete a thumbs-up. 'I'm going in!' he shouted.

He dropped overboard with the lifebelt in his hand and began struggling through the swirling, eddying water towards Clive. Pete leapt in behind him and fought towards the outcrop of slimy rock where Kieron stood sobbing.

Gwilym took a visual fix on Clive, registering from the crazy angles of his legs that they were broken. He moved close to the injured man and waited until he spun round, head foremost. The lifebelt went on in one clean sweep. Pete meanwhile had secured Kieron. As he moved the boy off the rock he saw the bag and the rifle. He picked them up and slung them over his shoulder.

Kieron was lifted on board the lifeboat first. Sydnie came forward and quickly wrapped him in a blanket. He clung to her, sobbing and shaking with the cold.

Together they watched as Clive, unconscious again, was hoisted up carefully on to the deck.

'Poor Dad,' Kieron whispered.

24

Edward Thorpe and Bob McGaskill sat by the telephone and radio desk in the crew room. They had already gone over the day's proceedings twice. They had discussed the merits of the applicants, agreeing that they all had what it took to do the job, more or less. Finally, they were at pains to reassure themselves that their judgement had been balanced and their final decision, though difficult to settle upon, had been completely sound. McGaskill looked at his watch, then at the silent radio. He yawned. They had run out of anything to talk about. Or McGaskill had. Thorpe was still curious about the woman. 'One thing puzzles me,' he said. 'Why is she so keen to change stations?'

'Let's just say a move was in everybody's interests.'

'Man trouble?' McGaskill shrugged. 'You might as well say, Bob. It won't affect anything now.'

'She got involved with a fellow crewman,' McGaskill said. 'A married crewman. His missus found out a few weeks ago and didn't take it lying down. So to speak.' He smiled thinly. 'Miss Hully realised she'd have to make a fresh start.'

Thorpe rolled his eyes. 'I hope that's not what she means by being one of the team. That's my worry, Bob. Men and women together, under a lot of pressure, in dangerous situations – it can easily lead to, well . . .'

'You're lucky to have her, Edward. She'll make a fine Senior Mechanic.'

Hughie and Sydnie were talking again in the forecabin as the lifeboat made its way back to Penrhys. They did not hear Geraint come in behind them.

'And the new boat, when it comes,' Hughie was saying, 'that'll be a challenge for you.'

'Let's get the appointment confirmed first,' Sydnie said, smiling.

Geraint lifted his foot and brought it down again sharply, announcing his presence. They turned and stared at him. 'When were you told?' he said, eyes slitted, nostrils wide under an imagined onslaught of conspiracy and betrayal. 'Before we launched? Before the interviews, even?'

'Geraint,' Hughie said, putting up his hand, 'don't be stupid.'

'Does everyone else on this boat know except me? Are they all laughing behind my back?'

'Edward Thorpe was going to talk to you when we got back on shore . . .'

'He had time to have his little talk with this one though.' Geraint jerked his thumb at Sydnie without looking at her. 'Thanks, Hughie. Thanks for the loyalty.'

He turned and stamped out of the cabin. Sydnie looked shaken.

'It's all right,' Hughie told her. 'That's just Geraint.' He got up and went out to look for him.

Geraint was hurrying along the deck, oblivious to the lights of Penrhys up ahead. He strode into the wheelhouse and stood beside Leslie at the wheel. Although he was choking with emotion, he strove nevertheless to look stoical and calm. 'I know you had a say in it,' he told Leslie. 'Don't pretend otherwise.'

Leslie glanced at him. 'If you're talking about the mechanic's job, I had no say whatsoever. I don't even know who's been bloody appointed.'

'Don't play games with me!' Geraint blinked back tears. 'I've been humiliated here – the least I deserve is some honesty.'

Leslie forced down his own rising emotion. He moved so his back was to Geraint, but Geraint put a hand on his shoulder, forcing him to turn back and look at him. 'Tell me why,' he demanded. 'Give me some reasons I can give to my wife and kids.'

Leslie blinked once, slowly. 'Don't you lay a hand on me on this boat,' he said. 'Not ever.'

Hughie appeared behind Geraint and eased him away. '*Dere mla'n nawr boi.* We'll be ashore in a minute. And you better cool down before you make a real fool of yourself.'

Geraint did not respond, but he let Hughie lead him out of the wheelhouse. They squeezed past Gwilym on his way in. He noticed how pale Leslie looked and asked if he was all right.

'I'm fine. Can you get on the radio and check we've got an ambulance waiting? Better call Doc Lewis, too, and get him to sedate that madman.'

'Geraint'll be OK,' Gwilym said. 'But I reckon we should call the police, anyway.'

He held up the shoulder bag Pete had lifted off the rocks at Pendragon Island. Opening it, he showed Leslie the dead chough inside. 'It wasn't just a day trip to Pendragon. He's a poacher.'

In the forecabin Hughie led Geraint to a seat and

told him he must make an effort to calm himself.

'I don't know how to face Dilys, Hughie. I honestly don't.'

'Thankfully, your Dilys has got more sense than you give her credit for. Listen, Geraint, you lost a job today, and that's tough. Very tough. But it was *my* job. Something I already lost and that I'll never ever get back.' He slapped Geraint gently on the shoulder. 'You'll find something else. You'll have another crack. I won't.'

Geraint took a long shaky breath, nodding, looking at his trembling hands. 'Sorry, Hughie.'

'Apology accepted, matter forgotten about.' Hughie smiled. 'This is my last shout, Geraint. I want to remember it for the good things.'

Within twenty minutes they were back on land. An ambulance with a flashing blue light waited as the boat was winched up; beyond the ambulance crew Barry Mitchell and another police officer stood watching, breathing plumes of steam into the air. Doc Lewis was inside the boathouse, talking to Dilys Gower as the crewmen disembarked.

Clive Hicks was taken on a stretcher to the ambulance. Kieron, swathed in a blanket, was brought in to sit beside him. Clive was under sedation, but his eyes were sunken with the kind of pain no drug can reach.

'We've been caught this time, eh, Dad?' Kieron whispered.

'I have,' Clive said, managing a smile. 'You've just been on a seaside holiday, all right, son?'

Kieron nodded and winked. He was chewing again, a large lump given to him by Sydnie. Making sure no one was watching, he pulled the gum in a string from his mouth and began winding it round his father's stretcher handle. 'We'll be back, Dad. Don't worry.'

The attendant climbed in beside them and closed the door. A moment later the ambulance started. Clive shut his eyes, holding tight to Kieron's hand.

Later that night George Bibby showed Barry Mitchell and Leslie into the room where Hicks and his son had stayed. He pointed to suitcases, a hold-all and several loose items under the table. 'There's all their gear.'

Barry picked up a large net fitted with ropes and pegs. 'This is what they call a whoosh net,' he said. 'It's for catching peregrines for the hawking trade. And that's a padded cage for transporting them.'

Leslie asked what kind of sentence Hicks was likely to get.

'Could be a fine of up to two thousand pounds for the dead chough. And he's got a record . . .'

Barry said an officer would call and collect all the Hickses' belongings in the morning.

'I knew I should have made him pay in advance,' George muttered as they left the room.

Downstairs in the bar Meryl was putting a pint of bitter and a whisky in front of Hughie. He paid her and looked around the place. Everyone was there, all the crewmen, all his old acquaintances, locked into their own conversations, taking no notice of him. Even Meryl had turned away as soon as he paid her. Hughie shrugged imperceptibly, determined to appear phlegmatic. You couldn't expect too much of an unfeeling world, he supposed. Warm farewells were old-fashioned. No going out with a bang, just the trace of a whimper.

As he put his glass to his lips everyone in the place turned towards him and began singing 'For He's a Jolly Good Fellow' at the top of their voices. Hughie was caught completely by surprise. He stood listening to them, grinning shyly, deeply moved. 'You daft buggers,' he grunted as they went into another chorus.

Leslie and George came into the bar. Leslie put his arm around Hughie's shoulder and joined in, singing louder than any of them.

The song ended with three rousing cheers. Sydnie entered from the foyer, clothes and hairstyle changed, looking very chic. Pete raised his glass and started singing 'For She's a Jolly Good Fellow', to her obvious embarrassment. The singing was taken up by Edward Thorpe, Hughie, Gwilym and Bob McGaskill.

A little way apart, Geraint and Dilys Gower sat at a table, watching the celebration.

Sydnie stood her ground at the bar, smiling, knowing beginnings were easy. Lasting was what counted. 'Thank you, thank you all,' she said as the singing ended. 'You're far too kind.'

She glanced aside and saw the cold looks from the Gowers, huddled across the room, isolated in their bitterness. She hung on to her smile, determined that in time she would fill the gap left by Hughie Jones, and earn the respect of the people of Penrhys. All of them.